"Why are you acting this way, Lije?"

Diana's voice held bewilderment—and fear. Lije had been so remote, so condemning lately. But she wasn't guilty of anything, except perhaps of loving him too much. Now it seemed as if she were going to lose him....

"Maybe I've come to my senses," Lije said harshly. "Maybe I've realized we can't spend the rest of our lives together."

It felt as if a knife had been twisted into her heart. "Are you saying our marriage was a mistake?" she breathed.

"One hell of a mistake." He turned abruptly. "Go pack your things. You can leave tomorrow. Have your lawyer get in touch with me."

She was still standing there like a statue when Lije walked out the door.

JANET DAILEY AMERICANA

LAND OF ENCHANTMENT

Harlequin Books

TORONTO • NEW YORK • LONDON
AMSTERDAM • PARIS • SYDNEY • HAMBURG
STOCKHOLM • ATHENS • TOKYO • MILAN

The state flower depicted on the cover of this book is yucca flower.

Janet Dailey Americana edition published September 1987
Second printing August 1988
Third printing August 1989
Fourth printing August 1990

ISBN 373-21931-8

Harlequin Presents edition published August 1976
Second printing January 1979
Third printing February 1982

Original hardcover edition published in 1975
by Mills & Boon Limited

CHAPTER ONE

"I'M OUT OF hair spray, Diana. Can I borrow some of yours?" Stella hovered behind the blond haired girl, taking care not to move her head too much for fear a brunet lock might slip out of place in her elaborate hair style.

"There." Diana pointed to an aerosol can on the table with the end of her eyebrow pencil before returning her concentration to the reflection in her makeup mirror.

Perfect, beautiful features stared serenely back. Large, luminous blue eyes that seldom revealed her inner thoughts were superbly framed by long curling lashes. Their thickness was increased now by the application of artificial eyelashes while a turquoise shade of eye shadow intensified the color of her eyes. Her nose was exactly right, not too short, not too straight, not too large. Her lips were proportioned correctly, too, with her upper lip forming a perfect cupid's bow; and the lower lip was just enough larger to appear sensuous under the application of layers of lipstick. She had an oval face and her creamy clear complexion was the envy of all the models. The pale ivory base makeup seemed wasted, since nothing could improve such a complexion.

From long experience, Diana added light feathery strokes of the charcoal gray eyebrow pencil to fill in and accent her finely arched brows. Removing the blue band that held her silvery blond hair away from her face, she began briskly brushing the long silken tresses. The ends of her hair curled naturally upward, including the bangs that she always brushed away from her face. She had been endowed with hair that naturally looked windblown and was beautifully rumpled when it actually was tossed around by the wind.

The door of the trailer swung open to admit a willowy chestnut-haired girl in a swirl of cool air. She shivered in her halter outfit as she quickly closed the door behind her.

"They're ready for you, Stella," she announced through chattering teeth.

"Tell them I'll be just a minute," Stella replied, inspecting her reflection for any last-minute adjustments.

"You tell them. I'm not going out there in that cold again until I have to," the other girl retorted sharply. "I'll never get adjusted to wearing summer clothes in the winter. I'll die of pneumonia first!"

"It's not usually this chilly in February, Vanessa," Diana reminded her.

Vanessa shrugged indifferently at that claim, choosing instead to call after the dark haired Stella just leaving the trailer, "Watch where you step or you'll be getting manure all over your shoes!"

Diana hid her smile at that warning, but not in

time for the disgruntled Vanessa to miss it. She let the glowering look slip by without comment.

"Wait until you get into that white outfit and have to wander around all those cows and horses with Connie shouting at you all the time not to get it dirty," Vanessa grumbled, slipping out of the brilliant flame-hued halter dress and into her long smock. "I don't understand how Connie comes up with these harebrained ideas. Whoever heard of clothes being photographed at a rodeo? It's positively ridiculous!"

"It is not ridiculous. It's a perfect background for this particular design blending Western and Indian with modern styles. What better place to do that than San Antonio, with its annual rodeo?" Diana reasoned, glancing away from the mirror long enough to see the thawing in Vanessa's face.

"Well, I will admit one thing. I've never seen so many good-looking, rugged he-men in one place before," the other girl relented. "And they aren't bashful about making their admiration known." Vanessa smiled at herself in the mirror. "I don't know when I've had so many whistles, winks, and invitations from the male sex."

"Don't let it go to your head." Diana warned. "You'll never meet a more footloose and roving bunch of men than these rodeo riders. They've got to be the land equivalent of the proverbial sailor with a girl in every port."

"You're always such a spoilsport." Vanessa shook her head sadly at the blond girl methodically brushing her hair until it glistened and crackled.

"Not every guy you go out with has to be the one you marry. There is such a thing as a fun date, you know. And I bet these cowboys can really swing!"

"You can have all the swingers as far as I'm concerned." Diana put the brush onto the little table and fluffed the ends of her hair with her hands. "You just point me to a nine-to-five man with a little home in the suburbs and I'll be happy."

"No one who's as domestically minded as you are should have been born with such looks. You're a disgrace to the modeling profession!"

"Don't be ridiculous!" Diane laughed. "I bet you sit home alone at night just as often as I do. You have to, or you wouldn't get enough sleep to keep those circles from clinging under your eyes or those inches from being added to your waistline from all the food and liquor."

"Being a model does have its limitations," Vanessa admitted reluctantly. "But that's just because we're here in Texas where the Miss America look is idolized. New York is a different story."

"Pooh!" Diana shook her head. "Dallas models are not any different from any high-fashion models you want to name. The work is just as hard and demanding, and not at all glamorous, as anywhere else, whether you're modeling clothes in a store or for a photographer as we do. And it's certainly not one big swinging party in any part of the country!"

"It does have prestige."

"I'd sooner have the prestige of being a wife and mother," Diana retorted, walking over to take the white jump suit off its hanger.

"Not me. I don't want some kid spoiling my figure."

Diana winced at that, the unfeeling statement hitting a wound that had never healed. But it was something she never discussed with anyone, mostly because there had never been anyone who had ever been close enough for her to confide in. She hid her loneliness behind the serene mask of beautiful composure and no one guessed it was there.

"Di, honey, what you need to do is go out a little more. It's about time you found out that there's more to life than marriage and kids."

Laughter rolled out easily at that superior remark. "You say it as though all I have to do is snap my fingers and I'll have a string of admirers standing at my door," Diana replied. "Do you know why I sat at home by myself on New Year's Eve? Because nobody asked me out. Everyone assumed that I was invited somewhere else. The nice guys in this world figure that a beautiful girl has all kinds of men ready and willing to date her, so they don't want to join the throng. Girls like you and me end up attracting the duds, the ones who need their images and egos boosted by being seen with a beautiful woman on their arm. They don't care anything about us as individuals."

"Lord! I never realized you were so bitter." Vanessa eyed her curiously. "You must have really been burned."

"A long time ago," Diana answered grimly, remembering the shock she had suffered when she discovered she was just a beautiful possession to a man she had liked very much.

It had hurt at the time, but now she could barely remember what he looked like. It hadn't really made her bitter, although she might have sounded that way. It only reaffirmed her desire to marry and settle down, but not with just anybody, only Mr. Right. At twenty-four, she was beginning to wonder if he would ever come along. Like everything else, Diana bottled that question inside her, keeping the poised, confident mask in place for the outside world.

"Oh, honey, you look beautiful in that!" Vanessa exclaimed as Diana locked the zipper in place and turned to inspect the slack jump suit in the full-length mirror.

The white fabric was one of those new lightweight synthetic knits that stretched and molded over a figure. There was only the slightest flare of the pants at her ankles before the material tightened at the knee and over the thigh to hug her waist, stretch over her breasts and around her neck in a halter, leaving her back bared. The striking feature of the outfit was the embroidered thunderbird design in bold turquoise colors that adorned the slack portion like a stripe up the side. It accentuated the blueness of Diana's eyes just as the white fabric complemented the pale color of her hair.

"You don't think it shows too much, do you?"

she asked, as she pulled the plunging V front closer together in an attempt to hide part of the cleavage of her breasts.

"Of course it does," Vanessa laughed, "but it's supposed to."

At that moment the trailer door opened again and an older, auburn-haired woman walked in. She was dressed in a tailored corduroy pantsuit with a heavy walking jacket. The rusty color accented the red in her hair. Glasses hung from a gold chain around her neck and there was a no-nonsense look in her face.

"Good," she said briskly, looking Diana over. "You're just about ready. Here's the jewelry that goes with that outfit."

Diana slipped the heavy turquoise and silver bracelet over her wrist and began putting on the matching earrings, aware of the scrutiny she was receiving from her employer, Connie Deveronne. After six years of modeling, the impersonal minute inspection still made Diana uncomfortable, but she never let it show.

"Have you been gaining weight?" Connie demanded in an accusing voice.

"No." Diana remained unruffled, knowing the scales had not changed in over three years, thanks to a closely watched diet.

"Your measurements are shifting, then." Her employer's eagle eye settled on the rounded curve of breast the low neckline revealed. "We're trying to sell the outfit and not your body. Are you wearing a brassiere?"

"Yes," she answered, keeping her eyes firmly averted and concentrating on the last earring being securely fastened. Only Diana knew that the light pink in her cheeks didn't come from any rouge.

"Take it off. It might flatten you a little to be without it." With that order given, Connie turned and walked toward the door. "Rick will be ready for you in about ten minutes."

"The old baggage!" Vanessa made a face at the door. "Doesn't she realize you're only going to look more sexy without it?"

"Haven't you realized that it's all right for us models to look sexy as long as it's the clothes we're wearing that make us that way," Diana laughed.

She couldn't admit how uncomfortably naked she felt without all of her undergarments. Vanessa would only laugh at her for being so prudishly modest and old-fashioned. Still, a few minutes later when Diana stepped out of the door of the trailer, she couldn't help thinking that all the eyes were turned her way were looking at only one thing. She forced herself to appear unconcerned, but her fluid movements were hurried as she subconsciously tried to escape the prying eyes.

The weather was cool. A sweater would have been welcome to cover her bare arms dappled with goose bumps. The nippy air made the animals frisky. Horses were prancing and pulling at their bits, snorting and sending puffy clouds of their frosty breath into the air. Halfway to where she was to meet the photographer, Diana met Stella on her way back to the trailer.

"How's it going?" Diana asked as Stella paused in front of her and turned to smile at a cowboy's complimentary whistle.

"Pretty good," Stella replied, glancing around quickly. "Connie's a little uptight because we're beginning to draw a crowd, but believe me, some of the looks will keep you warm."

"Hey, babe! What are you doing tonight?" A cowboy pulled his horse to a stop beside them and eyed Diana boldly.

"Sitting home with my sick mother," she answered easily. "Better luck next time."

The lean wiry figure wasn't at all put off by her weak excuse, but he tipped his hat and rode on. He hadn't really expected any different. Diana watched him for a moment before turning back to Stella and the knowing twinkle in her eyes.

"See what I mean?" Stella smiled. Diana raised her eyebrows in agreement before cattching sight of the auburn-haired woman approaching.

"I'd better get going. Here comes Connie now." Diana nodded toward the woman.

Connie Deveronne hustled Diana to where Rick, the photographer, waited. After only a few pictures, the young man lowered his camera, shaking his fair head. Connie was immediately at his side inquiring what was wrong.

"The white outfit needs a better background." The man looked around him searchingly. "Something with a bolder color, more defined."

Diana hovered to the side, shivering in the lightweight fabric. Patience was the byword of the model, with endurance coming in a strong second. She kept her attention focused on Rick and Connie, avoiding the cowboys seated on a nearby fence railing. She knew she was the object of their muffled laughter and whispering conversation. Dressed as she was, she felt singularly vulnerable.

"Come on, Diana," Rick called, "We're going to try the arena instead of these livestock pens."

Dutifully she joined them, seeing the cowboys out of the corner of her eye as they hopped down from their perch and joined the procession. If she hadn't been so ill at ease, it would have been amusing, especially considering the disgusted expression on Connie's face. It wasn't a long walk to the rodeo arena, but it wasn't made any shorter by the chill in the air. Diana hugged her arms around her shoulders to ward off some of it with her own body heat. The gesture brought an instant offer from one of the cowboys for Diana to take his jacket.

"Don't you dare put that smelly thing over that outfit!" Connie whispered threateningly.

As much as Diana would have liked to accept, she refused the offer with a smile of appreciation. Then they were all walking into the arena onto the red brown dirt. There were only a few horses and riders inside, but their entourage of cowboys quickly positioned themselves on the heavy wooden rails. Diana stood quietly as Rick and Connie discussed the situation, not paying too close attention until Rick let out a low whistle.

"That guy is straight out of a cigarette commercial," he murmured to Connie. "And have you ever seen a horse like that? This will be perfect!"

Even as Rick started walking forward, his hand raised in the air, Diana was trying to follow his direction. It only took her a second to see what had caught the photographer's eye. On the far side of the arena were a horse and rider cantering through a series of figure eights. The horse was blood red with flashy black stockings to above his knees and a black mane and tail. The man astride the horse was the personification of every publicity man's dream of a cowboy. He sat tall and erect in the saddle, each fluid movement of the horse matched by his own. The man was lean and tanned, dressed in faded blue Levi's with a matching denim jacket lined with sheepskin. And on his head he wore a weathered brown Stetson hat, pulled low over his face.

As the cowboy caught sight of Rick waving to him, he slowed his horse to a stop and walked in their direction. Diana watched as he sat immovable in the saddle and listened to Rick. Something in the man's bearing made her think that he would refuse to have himself and his horse act as a backdrop for Rick's pictures. There was the slightest hesitation before he looked to where Diana was standing beside Connie and nodded agreement.

Rick motioned her forward and Diana quickly complied. Precious time had been spent finding a suitable background, and Rick didn't waste any more of it making introductions between his model and the cowboy. Diana didn't even get a chance to study the man up close as Rick hurriedly moved her into position on the right side of the horse and began giving instructions. She was intrigued by the man atop the horse and in between snaps she sneaked quick glances in his direction.

Swift impressions were formed of a lean hard face, tanned and clean-shaven. The shadow of his hat brim made it difficult to determine the color of his hair, but Diana thought it was brown. His eyes were a different matter—one look they appeared blue and in another they were gray. Yet in all of her stolen glances one thing stood out, and that was his arrogant remoteness, as if all this was beneath his dignity. For some reason Diana wasn't offended by his coldness, which bordered on contempt. On the contrary, it fascinated her.

"Put your left foot in the stirrup," Rick ordered, his face concealed behind the black camera. "Stand in it suspended beside the horse."

Diana did as she was told, finding she had to hold on to the rider's shoulder to keep her balance. The sheepskin-lined jacket gave until it hit the solid muscle of his shoulder and arm. It was a strange sensation being so near this stranger. On the ground she had thought he was no taller than the average man, but now she realized she had made too much allowance for the horse. The man was tall, easily over six feet.

"Now, turn and look at him, Diana," Rick instructed.

His eyes were gray. She wondered how she had ever thought they were blue. They were slate gray—no, she reconsidered quickly. They were granite, as hard and unyielding as granite. Even the contours of his face were angular and uncompromising, too rugged to be handsome and too compelling not to be attractive. His masculinity was revealed in his strong features, just as his virility was in the sensuous line of his mouth. There was a slight bump in his otherwise straight nose that indicated that it had been broken at one time. But it didn't detract from his appearance. In fact, Diana discovered, it added to the look of an eagle about him, proud, commanding and free. Subconsciously she remembered that an eagle was a predatory bird.

His study of her had been just as thorough, only slightly less obvious. Then Diana noticed his gaze lingering on her low V neckline, and immediately her cheeks flamed with color. It didn't take an expert eye to determine that she was braless. Diana doubted that this man would be shocked by the discovery, but she was embarrassed by her own state. She knew the category men placed models in, and she had just reinforced it. When his gaze lifted to her eyes, she saw the look of amusement in it. But the amusement was generated by the flush in her cheeks.

Rick was shouting more instructions to her and Diana thankfully had to turn away. In seconds she was once more in command of her composure, although she was intensely aware of the man in the saddle. The thought kept running through her mind that she had never been so self-conscious in the presence of any other man. What was so different about this one? He was only a rodeo cowboy.

Just as Diana was striking another pose, one of the gates at the chutes swung shut with a loud bang. The blood bay horse that had stood with such restless restraint jumped forward, and Diana let out a startled gasp as she felt herself falling backward to the turf. But the man's reflexes were instantaneous. His right hand shot around her waist as his left drew on the reins to check his mount's flight.

In the span of seconds Diana was clutched tightly against his chest, held by the iron band of his arm. Her own arms circled his shoulders with her head buried beneath his chin. The closeness permeated her with the scent of his masculinity. She felt the flexing of his muscles as he controlled the horse and maintained his grip on her. The horse was stopped now, his head tossing in agitation and his hooves beating an in-place cadence.

The danger was over, but the blood still pounded in Diana's temples and her heartbeat had accelerated. She moved her head away from beneath the man's chin to stare wide-eyed into his calm face. Her waist was pinioned tightly against him, arching her closer. Only inches separated their faces. An invisible message was being exchanged by their eyes until Diana felt transformed by the wonder of it. His face remained as hard and remote as it ever was, but something had changed. Something had been transmitted between them and it was still tingling through her body.

"Are you all right?" His quiet voice seemed to come from a long way off.

"Yes," she breathed softly when she realized he was waiting for an answer.

Then they were no longer alone. Rick and Connie came rushing up to them, their concern dividing itself between Diana and the white jump suit. Effortlessly the man lowered her to the ground with one arm. Deprived of the warmth of his body, Diana shivered as she shrugged off her employer's inquiries. Connie turned her attention to the smudge mark on the knee of the slacks. The mark was too noticeable for any further photographs, but Rick consoled Connie with the fact that he thought he had sufficient. Diana was to return to the trailer and change.

The man was just reining his horse to leave when Diana stepped toward him. She had to tilt her head way back in order to look up into his impassive face. Her serene features were a mockery to the tumult she was experiencing inside.

"I want to thank you for saving me from that fall." It was amazing how composed her voice sounded. "I admire your expertise, Mr.—"

"Masters. Lije Masters." It was the first time Diana had ever seen anyone smile with his eyes. The line of his mouth never changed. The quiet respect stayed in his voice. But the corners of his eyes crinkled slightly and there was a glitter of light in the stone grayness of his eyes.

"Thank you, Mr. Masters," she said, feeling the

warm clasp of his hand take the one she had extended to him.

"My pleasure." Now mockery glinted as he touched his hat and turned the horse away.

Lije Masters. All the way back to the trailer the sound of it rolled silently on her tongue. It was an unusual name. Diana didn't recall ever hearing that first name before, but it belonged to an unusual man. She was sure that the last name was particularly apt. With his strength, he would be a "master" as an eagle was the ruler of the skies. Diana had never been so certain of anything in her life as she was that, above all else, she wanted to see Lije Masters again.

CHAPTER TWO

THE PHOTOGRAPHY SESSION lasted the rest of the afternoon. Diana dressed and undressed so many times that her shoulders and arms ached. The muscles around her mouth quivered from smiling so much. At every opportunity her eyes had scanned the collection of cowboys that roamed around, hoping to see the man on the blood bay horse. Once only had she seen him. It had been outside of the arena shortly after their initial meeting and he had been walking his horse toward the stable area.

Diana had believed that he would come to watch her work. By the end of the day, she realized Lije Masters wasn't the type to join the crowd of ogling cowboys. That brought up another question. How was she going to see him again? Connie Deveronne had brought her trio of models to San Antonio for a two-day session, Thursday and Friday. Tomorrow the pictures taken would be all wrapped up and on Saturday they would be traveling back to Dallas.

"Di, honey, you were terrific today!"

So lost in her thoughts was she, Diana jumped as Rick threw an arm around her shoulders and hugged her close to him. That was Rick, all professional during the sessions, only to turn into a wolf after they were done. He wasn't really a wolf, Diana amended, since wolves were dangerous. He was probably only a wolf cub. Rick liked to come on strong because he thought it was part of his image as a photographer. It was important to him to have a beautiful girl at his side, which was probably the reason Diana steered clear of him. She disliked the fact that it was her beauty that drew people toward her.

"Thanks for the compliment." She smiled coolly at him as she removed his arm from around her shoulders.

"Vanessa, Connie and I are going out tonight for dinner and all. Haven't had a chance to ask Stella what she's doing. Why don't the two of you join us?" Rick ignored Diana's attempt to put him off.

"It would be kind of tough dividing your attention between the four of us, wouldn't it?" she jeered softly.

"You'd be surprised at what I could do." His blue eyes roamed over her figure.

Diana didn't think she would be too surprised. She had made the mistake of going out with him once and discovered that after a couple of drinks Rick could turn into an octopus.

"No, thanks. I have other plans for tonight." Her refusal was brisk and firm.

"Don't tell me you're going to use those tickets the manager gave Connie for the rodeo?" He stared at her incredulously.

"The complimentary tickets, you mean?" Diana guessed astutely, a gleam of an idea already forming in her mind.

"What else? Come on, Di honey, you don't want to go to a corny rodeo tonight," Rick wheedled.

"There's where you're wrong." Diana smiled firmly, stepping quickly away from him to scurry to the trailer.

Once inside the small trailer, it took her searching gaze only seconds to find the tickets carelessly tossed on the counter. Diana knew Connie wouldn't give them another thought and quickly extracted two from the stack. Stella would be just as averse as she herself had been to spending an evening in the company of Rick, Vanessa, and Connie. With luck Diana could persuade her to attend the rodeo rather than spend the evening in their hotel room.

After a brief outburst from Stella that Diana had gone off her rocker, she warmed to the idea. Her one-track mind quickly remembered the admiring glances from the assortment of cowboys. Neither of them had had any previous inclination to attend such totally Western functions, despite the fact that they had both been born and raised in Texas. They were city girls and city girls are the same all over the world. Their planned night at the rodeo brought out a spirit of adventure in both of them. Of course, Diana's reason was completely different from Stella's. Hers was hinged on a man named Lije Master.

Their seats in the grandstand were strategically located near both the chutes and the gates where all the horsemen entered. Diana couldn't believe her luck. Her eyes searched the parade of riders during the presentation of the colors and the national anthem. There was not a sign of the blood bay horse and Lije Masters.

He had to be here, she told herself, switching her attention to the ever changing group of cowboys perched on the chutes and rails. The program called for saddle bronc riding first. Although Diana listened closely, she never heard his name called by the announcer. She applauded after each successful or unsuccessful ride, but not with the enthusiasm of her companion.

The next event was calf roping. Lije Masters was in the arena before Diana saw him. This time he was riding a sedate buckskin horse. Just watching him, she felt that odd breathlessness take hold of her chest. Her hands clapped for the roper completing his tie on a calf, but the only one that existed for her was Lije Masters.

"Our next contestant, ladies and gentlemen," the announcer was saying, "hails from the state of New Mexico—Elijah Masters!"

As soon as his name was announced, the rider set the now alert buckskin well back in the enclosure next to the tunnel chute. He gave a quick nod to a cowboy atop that chute and the door was pulled up and a hefty black calf came charging out. With a bounding leap the buckskin was after it. Diana saw the rope snake out from Lije's hand

and settle over the calf's neck in a perfect throw. With the precision of a trained athlete, the buckskin sat back on its haunches, the slack in the rope taken up in a few quick coils around the saddle horn. The calf was yanked off its feet as Lije vaulted out of the saddle in one fluid movement. He reached the calf just as it got back on its feet. He threw the animal to the ground, catching a front leg with his piggin string and making the tie with the back two legs before throwing his hands in the air to signal the official timer his completion.

There was a brief wait by the officials to make sure the calf couldn't free itself while Lije mounted the buckskin and rode it forward so the taut rope went slack. Diana joined in with the thunderous applause when it was announced that Lije Masters had the fastest time so far in that event. In response Lije removed his hat as he rode out of the arena, revealing thick, nut brown hair.

Diana's heart was in her throat as he neared the place in the entrance where she sat. Would he see her? Should she call to him? No, she couldn't do that. The last thing she wanted to have Lije think was that she was chasing him. The brown hat was on his head again when he did ride by Diana. The brim shadowed his eyes so that she had no way of telling whether or not he had seen her.

His calf-roping time didn't stand as another contestant riding the same buckskin horse that Lije had ridden beat him out of first place in the event by a full second. Bareback bronc riding was next, and again Lije didn't compete. Diana didn't see him again until the steer wrestling event, which the announcer explained was also known as "bulldogging." This time Lije was astride the red bay from that afternoon.

Lije Masters was one of the last contestants in the event, although he participated several times, acting as a hazer to keep the steer running straight so his competitor could vault from his horse and wrestle the steer to the ground. His big bay horse was used just as often.

When the moment came for Lije's attempt, Diana didn't know whether to cheer him on or hold her breath. The idea of him diving from his horse at a full gallop onto the horns of a big burly steer that was also running sent shivers of icy cold fear down her spine. She didn't have much time to dwell on it, because it was over almost before it began. Four strides out of the gate, Lije was off his horse, had the steer by the horns, brought it to a halt and had wrestled it to the ground. What was more important to Diana was that Lije was standing completely unharmed.

It frightened her how important this veritable stranger had become. It didn't seem natural, and yet she felt completely natural. Her concern and interest for Lije Masters was the most natural thing that had ever happened. There was the strange sensation that she had done this many times. And she couldn't explain why she felt that way.

This time when Lije rode out of the arena gate

he didn't continue on out of the stands as he had done before. He stopped his horse next to another cowboy who was leaning against the stands not too far from where Diana was sitting.

"With that big red horse of yours, you cain't never lose," the other cowboy laughed up at Lije, who stroked the glistening neck of his horse.

"That's the idea, Les. How's the ribs?"

"I'll tell you after the bull riding tonight. I drew that spinning devil," he answered grimly. "How about you?"

"I've got the gray," Lije replied.

"Watch him. He hooks to the left on a downed rider," the cowboy warned before he lifted his hand in a goodbye gesture and walked toward the back of the chutes.

Diana didn't understand what the conversation meant exactly. It sounded like serious advice. Her clouded blue eyes were studying Lije as he looked up and met her gaze. Again he touched his hat in that quaint Western way that Diana found pleasing. He inched his horse closer to where she sat.

"Enjoying the rodeo?" His drawl was not quite as pronounced as most that Diana had heard and there was a quiet, educated tone in his voice along with its natural commanding firmness. Lije Masters was a man who would be heard no matter how softly he spoke.

"Very much," Diana answered as she saw Stella glance at her curiously from the corner of her eye. "I've seen rodeos on television before, but it's the first one I've attended."

"I hope it won't be your last."

"I don't understand all the slang yet, but I've found it all very fascinating." Diana smiled. Her nerves were jumping as she waited anxiously for him to issue a more personal comment.

"There are a lot of things that happen behind the scenes that the spectators don't get to see. Later on when you're free, I'll show you around." The remoteness of his expression made it difficult for Diana to judge how sincere the invitation had been.

"I'd like that," she answered.

"If you'll excuse me, then, I have to get ready for the next event." Touching his hat, he reined the horse around and left.

"Do you know him?" Stella breathed after he was out of hearing.

"I met him today." Diana watched his retreating back until it disappeared.

"He's not really handsome, is he? I mean, not in the accepted sense of the word. But he's got an aura about him that takes your breath away. No wonder you wanted to come to the rodeo tonight!"

"What's the next event?" Stella's observation had been too astute and Diana wanted to shift the subject.

"Bull riding," Stella answered after consulting her printed program.

That was what Diana had been afraid it would be. And Lije Masters was entered in it. Her stomach twisted itself in knots. The apprehension she had felt during the steer wrestling seemed minor compared to the agony she knew she would go through in this, the most dangerous event.

"Are you going to do it?" Stella asked, her dark head cocked inquiringly toward her blond companion.

"Do what?"

"Take him up on his offer to show you around," Stella replied with a mock frown at Diana's blank expression. "I should think tonight after the rodeo would be a perfect time."

"Do you?" Diana asked earnestly before seeing the teasing look on her friend's face. Immediately she tried to appear nonchalant. "I haven't made up my mind yet."

"We're only going to be here for another day." The dark head shook sadly. "This isn't the time to play hard to get, Di."

"I just don't want it to look as if I'm chasing him." she sighed.

"He issued the invitation. It's up to you to accept. I just wish he had a friend for me!" A resigned smile played across Stella's face.

"Oh, you're coming with me," Diana said quickly.

"I would make it a crowd. No, thanks." Stella shook her head firmly. "And if you're getting cold feet about accepting that date, then you're a fool."

Diana knew Stella was right. She knew, also, that she was going to accept the offer, but that didn't ease her tension. She hadn't even been this much on edge when she received her first kiss. Some inner voice told her that this was the most important evening in her life, and she couldn't be as blasé about it as Stella was.

Bull riding was an event that Diana watched with fascinated horror. The cowboys who were able to stay on the vicious-looking bulls for the required eight seconds still had to get off. In this event there were no pickup men on horses in the arena. The only protection the rider had was the clowns in their baggy pants and painted faces. Diana's terror was so strong that she couldn't even join in with the rest of the audience as they gasped, then laughed at the daring antics of the brave clowns, who by one means or another diverted the bull's attention from the defenseless rider.

It was worse when Lije was announced. The fear of watching the spectacle was not as great as the fear of not watching. He went the full eight seconds on the twisting, bucking, spinning, angry bull, a giant of a beast with a big hump on its neck and an evil face. As the buzzer sounded, Lije slipped from the bull's back. It spun around, hooking its huge horns to the left as Lije dodged out of danger to the right. Diana's heart didn't start beating again until he was safely astride the fence.

There were only two riders left after him, and for Diana they were an anticlimax. The man she had only met that afternoon had made his ride safely. Although all the cowboys who participated were virtually strangers to her, he was the only one that mattered in a personal way to her.

The rodeo was over and the grand exodus of the audience began. This was the moment Diana had been looking forward to and dreading. She smoothed the crease on her lavender slacks, straightened the matching box jacket, and touched the turtleneck of her white ribbed sweater. Moistening her lips with her tongue, she looked over at the girl standing beside her.

"Do I look all right?" she asked anxiously.

"With anyone else, I'd think you were angling for a compliment," Stella laughed. "That cowboy has really got you, hasn't he?" A spot of pink appeared on Diana's cheeks as she tried to ignore the teasing statement. "You look fine," Stella smiled. "You'll knock him out and you know it. Now, run along. I'll see you later at the hotel and you can give me all the delicious details."

Diana reluctantly left her companion and walked in the opposite direction of the parking lot. The streetlights did their best to illuminate much of the darkness, but even in their light it was difficult to distinguish the features of people who were more than a few feet away. Diana had only a general idea of where to look for Lije, and that was in the stable area. She was hesitant to ask the numerous other cowboys who were around where to find him lest they mistake the reason for her interest in them.

For several minutes she walked around by the stables area hoping to get a glimpse of Lije Masters. But after ignoring another query as to what she was doing that night and wouldn't she like to join the asker, Diana realized that her silence was getting her nowhere. The only way she was going to find Lije was to ask for him.

"Excuse me," She chose an older-looking cowboy with bowlegs and a kind face. "I was wondering if you could help me."

"Be glad to." He smiled, stopping a few feet in front of her. He was lean and wizened, not much taller than Diana herself, who was five foot six.

"I'm looking for Lije Masters. I was wondering if you could tell me where I might find him."

"Shore thing, ma'am. You go to the second row of stables and turn right. He'll be somewhere in the middle."

After thanking the cowboy for his help, Diana set off in the direction he gave. The unhappy thought kept running through her mind that Lije might have already left the rodeo grounds as so many of the cowboys were doing. When she rounded the corner of the second row of buildings, she experienced a mixture of relief and trepidation at the sight of several groups of cowboys standing near the stalls.

As she walked by the clusters of three or more men, Diana heard their loud voices fall to whispers and finally silence when she went by. Her gaze furtively searched their midst for the tall, lean man she was looking for, but she made it a point not to meet the bold gazes. She kept a purposeful step to her walk as if she knew exactly where she was going. Her lack of any noticeable attention to the cowboys kept any passing comments between those in the group. The next group Diana wasn't able to sidestep as easily.

"Hey, Blondie!" one of the men called to her as she approached. She tilted her head away from him after she had determined that it definitely wasn't Lije Masters, but the cowboy wasn't deterred that easily. "You gotta be lookin' for me, baby, because I'm the only one around here that's got any day money in his pockets." He planted himself cockily in her path and moved to block her when she would have gone around him. "You are some sexy blonde," he stated, surveying her from head to foot.

"Excuse me, please," she said with angry patience, but he still wouldn't let her by.

"Say, I've seen you. You were one of those models that was strutting around here this afternoon. Listen, doll face, why don't you and me go have a drink somewhere?"

This time Diana met his stare with a cool and contemptuous one of her own. The cowboy was young and very obviously good-looking—too much so, since it had given him a very swelled head.

"I'm meeting someone. Would you please let me by?" she repeated.

"Baby, there ain't no one around here that could possibly be better than me," he assured her. A devilish twinkle was in his eyes as his friends behind him sniggered at that statement.

"I choose my own escorts," Diana retorted with deliberate, cutting coldness.

"You've cornered yourself a fiery little filly, Jack," one of the men hooted.

It was an unpleasant situation. Diana could see the brazen cowboy reassessing his chance of success. She had learned long ago that calm indifference combined with a few well-chosen words usually put off the most persistent wolves.

"I might have known you would be the one to waylay my girl, Evans."

A third voice startled both Diana and the cowboy blocking her way. A sigh of relief sounded from Diana as she recognized Lije Masters walking toward them. His arrival brought a swift end to the cowboy's desire to prolong the conversation. There was a hint of a smile around his mouth as Lije met the grateful look she gave him. The cowboy named Evans was already moving to the side.

"The lady never said she was meeting you, Masters." The wind was out of the cowboy's sails and Diana was glad.

Her heart was still singing with the words "my girl," although she realized they were said for someone else's benefit.

"I was wondering what kept you, Diana." Lije Masters smiled and the smile removed all the hard remote lines in his face. Diana felt bathed in a golden glow of warmth that increased as his hand took her elbow and guided her away from the group of silent cowboys. When they were out of earshot, he looked down at her, his gray eyes twinkling with amusement. "It is Diana, isn't it?"

"Yes. Diana Mills." Breathless embarrassment crept into her throat, making speaking difficult. She felt so strangely submissive when she was with him. "I have to thank you again for rescuing me."

"It was my pleasure again." The smile was no longer on his lips but had retreated to his eyes. And Diana regretted the loss. "I was settling my horses for the night. It'll take a few more minutes. Do you mind?"

"Not at all," Diana replied, trying hard not to feel she was superfluous.

The buckskin and the bay were in adjoining stalls not too far from where Lije had found her. The stalls were large and roomy, but Diana stayed by the door. She had never been very comfortable around horses, mostly because she hadn't had too much to do with them. She was content to watch Lije as he picked up a curry comb and began brushing the broad back of the dappled buckskin.

"What are the names of your horses?" Diana asked, noting the ease with which he moved around the horse.

"This fellow," he answered, slapping the buckskin on the side to get him to move over, "is just plain Buck. Red, my other horse, is registered with the American Quarter Horse Association as Firebrand."

Diana watched while Lije picked up the horse's hoof and began cleaning it. It made her wonder if she could ever behave that naturally with a horse. That thought made her laugh silently, because where would she ever have the chance to find out?

"Why do you have two horses?"

The gray eyes smiled at her question as Lije lifted the last hoof and cradled it on his knee.

"Buck is the best all-around horse a man could have. He ropes calves, does a good job of hazing, serves as a pickup horse if he's needed, can cut and rein as well as any, and in a pinch you can bulldog off him. For steer wrestling, nothing can touch Red." He set the hoof back on the floor. "There, all done."

Brushing the straw from his tan dress jeans, Lije walked to the stable door where Diana was standing. His shadow loomed over her momentarily before he stepped into the outside light.

"There's not really a lot I can show you this late." It wasn't an apology, but the statement of a fact that they were both aware of. "There's a little café down the street. Would you like some coffee?"

Diana agreed. But later when they walked into the brightly lit restaurant, she wished he had chosen somewhere a little less public. Looking across the table at him, it was hard for her to believe that she had ever been crushed against that broad chest. It was hard to believe any of this was happening to her. She couldn't think of anything to say and she never remembered being this tongue-tied on any date. She felt embarrassed telling the waitress that she wanted her coffee black.

"Are you from San Antonio?" Lije was leaning back in his chair, his long legs stretching beneath the table. If Diana seemed uneasy, Lije appeared totally relaxed and in command—which he was.

"No, I'm from Dallas. I grew up there and except for a few weekend excursions I really haven't been anywhere. That probably sounds very dull to someone like you who travels all over the country." Diana nervously clasped her hands around the heavy mug of coffee.

"Not quite what you would expect from a model," he agreed dryly.

"Modeling is just like any other job or profession. It may sound glamorous, but it's really a lot of hard work and self-discipline."

"Don't you enjoy it?" An eyebrow rose briefly over a gray eye.

"I...I like it well enough."

"What made you decide to become a model?"

"It seemed the only logical choice at the time," Diana sighed, taking a slip of the hot liquid. "I didn't seem suited for anything else. Education costs money."

"What about your parents? Couldn't they help?"

"I have no parents." Camouflaged defiance made her look at him boldly. "I'm your typical baby on the doorstep."

His gaze made a slow study of her face. There was authority in his expression, but Diana couldn't detect any patronizing air of superiority.

"You were never adopted?"

"I was very sickly as a baby and a child," Diana replied. "My earliest memories are of hospitals and doctors and nurses. By the time I got over all the illnesses, I was too old. People only want to adopt babies or children under five. So I had a succession of foster parents, which was nice, because I always had a room of my own."

"I imagine if you were as beautiful then as you are now, it must have been difficult for you."

Diana glanced at him in surprise. "How did you know? Most people think it made it easier."

"Generally children are placed in homes where there are the children almost the same age. It would be logical for the natural children of your foster parents to be envious and even jealous of you." Lije reasoned.

"Yes. It really complicated things. The parents tried to be objective, but it was hard for them, too. I mean, all parents like to believe that their child is the prettiest or the most intelligent." All the little long-ago hurts brought a haunting quality to her expression. "The last family I stayed with had a daughter just a few months younger than myself. When I first came there she had a steady boyfriend, but just by my being there, they broke up. I never did anything to make him think I was interested in him. It was really awful. He kept calling me on the phone. She was really a nice girl, and I would have liked to have had her as a friend."

"What made you decide to take up modeling?"

"It seemed obvious. After all, how many bosses' wives would want someone like me as their husband's secretary?" Diana smiled. "As I said, I didn't have the money to go on to college even if I could have got a partial scholarship. I went to work in a department store in Dallas Within a month I was modeling some of their clothes, which was when Connie Deveronne saw me. She's my employer now.''

''What would you have done if you were able to choose?''

''I think I would like have liked to be a teacher in the primary grades or preschool.'' She stared wistfully at her coffee.

CHAPTER THREE

"WELL," DIANA BREATHED in deeply, "I've managed to give you my life history. Now tell me about yourself. I know you're a rodeo rider and come from New Mexico."

She liked the amused glint that came into his eye. Did he guess that she had changed the subject so she wouldn't reveal how really empty and lonely her life had been?

"That about sums it up," Lije stated with infuriating calm.

"Are you married? Single? What about your parents? How long have you been riding in rodeos?" Diana lightly rattled off a list of questions, hoping she didn't betray her intense interest in his answers.

The corners of his mouth lifted in a faraway, indulging smile. "I'm thirty-one years old and unmarried, which is the only way a man should follow the rodeo circuit with any success. My mother died when I was seven and my father a few years ago. I started out competing in high school rodeos, but I've been competing in RCA-sanctioned rodeos off and on for the past twelve years."

"What does RCA stand for?"

"Rodeo Cowboys Association. Do you want any more coffee?" At his adept change of subject Diana realized that Lije was as reticent to discuss his past as she had always been.

She declined the coffee and rose when he did to leave. They strolled leisurely back to the stable area, ignoring the cold bite of the night breeze as Lije shortened his long stride to match hers.

"Why do you ride in rodeos?" Diana glanced up at him curiously.

"It's probably the cleanest sport there is. Although the spectator thinks of it as man competing against man, it really is a battle between man and animal. Not a life-and-death struggle like bullfighting, but a pitting of skills against a clock."

"Isn't it cruel, though, to the animals?"

"Hardly," Lije answered, chuckling softly. "In the first place, I don't recall ever seeing a horse treated for anything more severe than a strained muscle, unless it accidentally got tangled in the chutes; but I wouldn't even want to attempt to count the number of riders who've suffered broken bones or internal injuries. The odds are with the animals basically. I don't think there's a town where a rodeo plays that there aren't half a dozen or more representatives from the Society for the Prevention of Cruelty to Animals haunting the grounds. There are horses that are born to buck, just like some are born to run."

"Tonight I heard one of the cowboys tell you something about the bull you were to ride."

"Riders always pass along information to one another concerning the characteristics of an animal. You'll always see some cowboy helping another in the chutes or acting as a hazer in the steer wrestling or calf roping. As I said, you compete with the animal and the clock, not each other."

"Why do you ride?" Diana asked, aware that he had dodged any specific answer before.

"Why do you model?" he returned.

"For money."

"That's why I'm here in San Antonio."

"Don't you ever want to settle down? I mean, you can't rodeo ride forever." She tried hard to see his expression in the dim light.

They took several steps before he answered her. When he did, Diana had the thought that he had weighed each word carefully before answering.

"Another two years on the circuit and I'll be able to quit—as long as nothing changes," Lije said firmly— too firmly for it to have been for her benefit.

"What would change?" She glanced up to his face as they passed beneath a streetlight. The harsh expression in his eyes startled her before he turned his face away.

"Nothing will," he stated.

"After two years, what then?"

"I'll go back to my ranch in New Mexico."

"If you own a ranch, then why are you here? Surely you should be there running it." They were walking past the stables to some parked vehicles.

"I can't afford it." Lije answered grimly.

"Eleven years ago, when my father was alive, we had a drought that just about wiped us out. It took a couple of years with me riding in rodeos and him working on the ranch to get it together again. I kept riding so we could make improvements to the place. Then three years ago he died and I got hit with all the inheritance taxes. I had to go back on the circuit to make ends meet."

His steps had ceased and unknowingly Diana had stopped, also. His last statement explained a lot of things. Lije Masters was a man with roots, with a heritage and pride that made him stand out from the other rodeo cowboys she had seen who lived blithely for the day with no thought of tomorrow.

"It's not much for transportation," Lije said, lifting a hand towards a battered pickup truck parked in front of them. "But I think it will make it to your hotel. Where are you staying?"

"At the Hilton," Diana replied, accepting his helping hand into the cab and smiling her thanks as he made sure the door closed fast. After he had started the pickup and pulled onto the street she said softly, "You must miss your ranch very much."

"I do."

"Would you tell me about it?" she asked.

The gray eyes swept over her face, studying the extent of her interest.

"It's in the mountains northwest of Socorro, New Mexico. The Continental Divide bisects one corner of the ranch and the lava beds are to the north. It's miles from the nearest neighbor or town. We run mostly sheep right now, although we've started changing to cattle. It will be a while before the herd builds up, which is just as well since it would be hard for one man to handle both. Jim—the two of us were raised together like brothers—is taking care of it now for me. It's beautiful country." He glanced at her briefly. "Wild, rugged mountains covered with pines and lush green valleys. Sometimes I get hungry just for the sight of it."

The warmth in that brief look made Diana swallow. Lije seemed more remote than he had ever been. As he had been describing the ranch to her, she could tell he was picturing it in his mind. She realized that there was no sacrifice too large for him to make to keep that land. Born and raised in the city, Diana knew nothing about ranches, cattle, horses, or anything that was a part of Lije Master's life. It was frightening to think of how little they had in common. Thankfully, Lije didn't seem to expect her to make a comment about the ranch he had just described, and Diana was able to nod and smile.

Her hotel was directly ahead of them. Lije parked the truck along the curb and Diana studied his carved profile as he turned off the motor. She admired the strength of purpose that was etched there, because she knew the cost he paid. When he turned toward her she wanted to reach out and touch him, give him some of the softness that he had been denied, but it was impossible to do.

"How long will you be staying here?" Lije asked, propping his elbow on top of the steering wheel as he leaned against his door.

"The photographs are supposed to be finished tomorrow," Diana admitted reluctantly. "We'll probably go back to Dallas on Saturday. What about you?"

"After Sunday's performance I'll be heading on to Houston."

Diana shivered—not from the cool air. The thought that in less than two days they would both be in separate parts of the state and maybe never see each other again made her feel cold inside. Their paths had just crossed momentarily.

"I suppose I'd better go in," she sighed, not able to think of anything else to say that would prolong their conversation.

"Will you be going to the rodeo tomorrow night?" Lije made no move to follow up her suggestion.

His question had caught Diana off guard. "Yes, I thought I would." Actually she hadn't progressed that far in her plans.

"I'll probably see you then." This time his hand did reach down for the door handle and he opened the door and stepped out of the truck.

Diana shook her head. She had honestly expected him to make a date to see her, but he had left it to a "maybe." With his impassive face, it was impossible to tell whether he even wanted to make that "maybe" become a fact. There was a constriction in her throat as she took the hand he offered her out of the truck. He didn't walk her to the hotel, but stood on the sidewalk.

"Good night, Diana," he said, touching his hat, his gray eyes smiling.

"Good night, Lije."

The area was well lit. People were walking along the pavement behind them. A more personal good night wasn't possible, and Diana sensed that Lije had arranged it this way. Before she turned to walk toward the hotel, he was already walking back to the driver's side of the car.

Stella was awake when Diana entered their hotel room. She was sitting up watching one of the late shows on television. Upon her friend's entrance she switched off the set and turned expectantly to Diana.

"How did it go?" Stella asked eagerly.

"Fine." Diana slipped off her jacket and hung it up before sitting down in front of the little vanity to begin brushing her long, silver blond hair.

"Fine? Is that any way to describe an evening? What did you do? Where did you go?"

"We went to a restaurant, had some coffee, talked, and he drove me home." Diana shrugged, knowing how unbelievably dull that sounded.

"Are you serious?" Stella squeaked, sitting upright in the bed and hooking her dark brown hair behind her ears. "There had to be more to it than that! He did kiss you, didn't he?"

"No, he didn't," Diana replied sharply, setting the brush back on the table before she had completed her customary one hundred strokes.

"Oh, Di, I always knew you were slow." Her friend shook her head sadly at her. "But we're only going to be here for another day. You just don't have time for three dates before a guy kisses you."

"It does take two, you know!" Diana pushed the blond hair away from her face and took a deep breath to control her rising temper. "I'm going to see him tomorrow."

"Then did he ask you out?"

"Not exactly." Diana sighed, turning her bewildered gaze on her friend. "Stella, I just don't understand him. It's infuriating. He makes a point of asking if I'm going to the rodeo tomorrow night. When I say that I am, he says he'll probably see me. And that big cowboy doesn't even sound as if he cares!"

"It's obvious that you do." Stella leaned back against the pillow and studied Diana thoughtfully.

"I've just met him." Diana tried to sound offhand and she failed. "I don't know. I don't understand why he's so important to me."

"I wouldn't let it bother you," said Stella, punching her pillow and slipping under the covers. "That man has a chemistry about him that attracts. If you hadn't seen him first, I would have snatched him up for myself tonight."

Sighing as she undressed and got ready for bed, Diana didn't think the answer was quite as simple as Stella thought. If she was honest with herself, she didn't want it to be that simple.

THE FOLLOWING DAY's photography session seemed to last forever. Diana had never known the hours to drag so badly. Her attention wasn't on her work because her eyes kept searching the crowds for some sign of Lije Masters. More than once Rick spoke sharply to her while Connie tossed daggers with her eyes. She was so depressed by the end of the day because she hadn't seen a trace of Lije that after she had scrubbed her face clean of all its heavy makeup she didn't even have the energy or desire to apply light touches of mascara and lipstick.

Wearing a blue windbreaker over a pair of scruffy white slacks, she dejectedly followed Stella from the trailer. From habit, her eyes traveled over the distant group of cowboys along the route to the parking lot. She was so busy trying to identify the faraway figures that she wasn't conscious of the horse and rider approaching them, not until the man was abreast of them and Stella poked her sharply in the ribs.

"Hello, Diana."

She stared in disbelief at the man reining his horse in beside her. The gray eyes looked calmly back. She had to swallow several times to get her voice to work.

"Hello, Lije," she replied in a small tight voice.

"I'll see you at the car," Stella said, stepping away quickly to leave them alone.

"Are you through for the day?" he asked.

"Yes." Her hand went nervously to her hair as Diana realized she probably looked pale and colorless without any makeup, unaware of the sparkle that lit her eyes or the glow of pleasure that shone from her face. "We...we were just heading back to the hotel."

"I almost didn't recognze you without the war paint." His gaze swept over her face with arrogant coolness, the light in his eyes indicating that he saw the spreading pink shade in her cheeks. "I think you look more attractive this way."

"Thank you." Diana lowered her gaze. Here was a compliment that she couldn't brush off as she had so many others from different people. This one came from Lije and it was special.

"Would you like to have dinner with me tonight after the rodeo?" he asked suddenly.

"That would be nice," she agreed quickly, swallowing back the lump of happiness in her throat to smile up at him.

He nodded and started to turn his horse away to leave, then stopped to look down at her again. "Meet me at the stables about seven and I'll show you around."

Diana was too happy to take offense at the way he had put it as an order and not a request.

"I'll be there," she assured him as he touched his hat and nudged his horse into a canter.

She nearly floated to the parking lot where Stella waited. Her companion didn't need to ask what had caused the bemused expression on her friend's face. It was just as well, because Diana was too wrapped up in her own happiness to talk.

At seven she was still walking on air as she

rushed to meet Lije at the stables. It wasn't the hurrying that had caused her breathlessness. Diana had chosen her outfit with care—a blue denim slack suit that deepened the color of her eyes and offset the fairness of her pale hair. She had been just as careful applying the light makeup, since Lije had made it clear he liked the natural look. Her appearance must have pleased him because she was rewarded with one of his rare smiles that so completely transformed his remote features.

Lije kept his word, taking her all around the adjoining rodeo grounds, pointing out everything he thought would be of interest to her. Diana was too dazzled by her companion to take more than a cursory interest in most of it, though she did manage to absorb enough to ask intelligent questions when the occasion demanded it.

Much too soon for Diana came the time for the grand entrance. He led his buckskin to the arena gates with Diana walking beside him. There was a thrill of belonging when an official started to stop her and Lije spoke up quickly that she was with him and she was allowed in. Handing the reins of his horse to another cowboy, he took her by the arm and led her to the side toward an older, battered-looking cowboy on crutches.

"I want you to stay here with Lefty," Lije commanded gently. "He'll keep you out of trouble and tell you the finer points of rodeoing."

"All right," Diana agreed, liking the protective and possessive way those gray eyes were looking at her. Even better she liked the way they sharply turned on the short, lean cowboy.

"Take care of her." Lije told him.

"You bet. If anybody comes near her, I'll chase 'em away with my crutch," the cowboy assured him with pseudoferocity.

Lije's hand touched her shoulder lightly before he walked back to his horse. In one lithe movement he was astride, his boots automatically finding the stirrups. Diana would have been content to watch him, but the older man was already claiming her attention.

"Lije didn't see fit to introduce us," he was saying. "My name's Lefty Robbins."

Diana shook the callused brown hand he held out to her, aware that now that Lije was gone she was undergoing a close scrutiny.

"Well, Diana," said Lefty after she had told him her name, "let's wander over to the stands behind the chutes. You can get a good look-see there."

There was no choice but to follow him, although once they had reached their vantage point she had to admit he had chosen well. There was an unobstructed view of the chutes and the arena.

"What happened to your leg?" Diana asked as she watched him gingerly lower himself to the seat, making sure his leg was stretched out comfortably.

"Ah, a fool horse kicked me out in the stables and fractured an old break," he replied gruffly. "I was doin' pretty good up till then."

"That's hard luck," she commented sympathetically.

"Heck! If it weren't for bad luck, I wouldn't have no luck at all." His weathered face twisted into a smile, "That's how I got my name."

"Lefty? I don't understand."

"My left arm has been broken over a dozen times. The boys were going to chip in and buy me a permanent cast," he chortled, and Diana's blond head tilted back to join his laughter.

Just as the night before, after the parade and the national anthem the first event was saddle bronc riding. The winning ride was by the cowboy who had stopped Diana in the stables, Jack Evans. His swagger was even more pronounced than it had been when she had met him.

"Why doesn't Lije ride bucking horses?" she asked, turning to Lefty as they cleared the arena for the calf roping.

"He's too big. A good bronc rider is usually lean and only average height. You gotta be small and wiry like me to stay on those sun-fishin' horses," Lefty announced proudly. "Not that Lije couldn't stay on; he just couldn't rack up the points with any consistency. Now bull ridin' is something different. It's still better to be smaller, but he can use his strength to make the ride. Lije may not make day money in the event, but he'll end up somewhere in the placings."

"What's day money?"

"A cowboy rides in a particular event every night. The one with the highest score, like in bronc and bull ridin', or the fastest time for calf ropin' or steer wrestlin', wins that day's prize money. But the scores accumulate each day so that at the end of the rodeo the cowboy who's consistently done the best in a particular event gets the big prize.''

Diana's questions set off a running commentary from Lefty as he explained the various technicalities of each event. He pointed out the string barrier that allowed the calf a head start before the roper was permitted to go after him. If the roping horse broke the barrier, there was a ten-second penalty added to his roping time. After the catch had been made, the calf had to be on its feet before the cowboy could throw it back on the ground and tie its feet.

It continued on through the bareback-riding event, where Lefty told her that the rider had to have his feet above the horse's shoulders as the horse came out of the chute or he was disqualified. The rider's free hand could never touch the horse, which was the reason he waved it in the air above him so the judges could see he didn't touch the horse, as well as to give him a certain amount of balance.

"Why does Lije let other cowboys ride his horse?'' Diana asked as the steer wrestling began.

"He don't exactly 'let' them ride his horse,'' Lefty smiled. "You see, Lije's got himself a valuable piece of horseflesh there, 'cause it's probably the best dogging horse around. Them boys pay to use his horse, so much for each go-round or a percentage of the purse if they win on him. That red horse of his makes Lije a pretty fair profit. I don't know how many offers he's had to buy that stallion, but the price is going up in the five-figure range now. That Lije Masters has a pretty smart head on his shoulders.'' He winked confidentially at Diana. "With that horse and Lije's own natural know-how, those two could take it all this year and end up at the National Finals Rodeo in Denver.''

Lefty fell silent during the bull-riding event, sensing the reason for Diana's clenched hands and pale face. After Lije's successful ride she smiled weakly at the older cowboy, who nodded and patted her hand comfortingly before signaling that it was time for them to leave and meet Lije.

CHAPTER FOUR

LEFTY PERSUADED LIJE that even with his rstricted mobilty he was capable of taking care of the horses. Lije agreed to the offer, although he unsaddled them before they left.

"Would you mind waiting a few minutes outside my camper while I change my clothes?" Lije asked as he and Diana walked toward some parked vehicles near the stables. He glanced ruefully at the dirt stains on his white shirt. "I forgot to tell the bull I was taking you out to dinner."

"I don't mind waiting," Diana laughed as they stopped beside a pickup truck with a camper mounted in the bed and over the cab.

"I won't be long," he promised, adding with an impish twinkle, "I would invite you in, but...."

"I'll wait outside." A rising tide of warmth started up her neck. She had been in those types of campers before and knew very well there wasn't any real privacy when it came to dressing and undressing. A smile crinkled his eyes as he nodded and entered the trailer.

True to his word, Lije was out in a matter of minutes. He hadn't just changed his shirt, though, but his entire dress. Now he was wearing a

Western-cut suit of brown corduroy with an open-neck shirt in a cream yellow. The outfit enhanced his rugged good looks, intensifying the color of his gray eyes while it complemented his dark brown hair and accentuated the width of his shoulders and the slimness of his hips. Lije Masters looked every inch the commanding rancher, and the effect awed Diana.

"Will I do?" he asked mockingly as she continued to stare at him.

"Now I'm the one who feels she should change," Diana laughed nervously, glancing down at her suddenly plain denim slack suit with its white stitching.

"It's too late. I'm hungry," he decreed, taking her arm and guiding her to the front of the truck. "And you would attract attention no matter how you were dressed. I don't think any man would ever look to see what you were wearing."

"I'll take that as a compliment," she murmured, a little overwhelmed by this charming side of Lije Masters.

"Good," he responded, holding the door as she climbed into the cab. "That's the way I meant it."

There was a caressing quality to his softly spoken words that quickened her pulse. All day she had been wondering how she could get close to this remote and sometimes arrogant man, but Diana was learning fast that it was he who set the pace of their relationship. She could only follow his lead. She had always resented anyone who was dominant or dominating to others, including herself, but this time she thought it would be nice for Lije to rule her.

The restaurant he took her to had a friendly, informal atmosphere; it was decorated with Western trappings that were a perfect background for Lije. Last night Diana had discussed her past with him with ease and tonight she found herself doing it again. Lije Masters had the rare quality of being able to listen with sincere interest and draw people out with gentle, probing questions, while Diana learned little more about him than she had before. After their meal was finshed, she switched the position.

"Tell me how the son of a rancher came to be named after the Biblical prophet Elijah?"

The corner of his mouth lifted in a half smile as he studied his coffee for a minute before looking up to meet her frank gaze. There was a velvet quality to the color of his eyes that was oddly soothing.

"My father's name was Daniel, a common name, although it's found in the Bible. But my mother, Naomi, was a religious woman. She had had several miscarriages before, in her middle thirties, I came along. Elijah was considered a messenger of glad tidings in the Bible and lived in the mountain wilderness, and she felt it was doubly appropriate. My father was the one who shortened it to Lije."

For the first time in many years Diana was struck by the sadness that she would never be able to recount personal stories like that. When she was left at the orphanage there hadn't even been a note telling her name.

"You haven't said when you're leaving tomorrow," Lije stated when Diana didn't speak.

"I don't know," she sighed, giving herself a mental shake to remove the slight depression. "There's a chance we won't be leaving—something about Rick wanting some action shots. Connie was supposed to let us know this evening."

"Should you phone the hotel?"

"She'll tell Stella if I'm not there." Diana glanced at her watch. "I probably should call Stella, though, so she won't have to wait up for me to let me know."

"You do that, while I take care of the check."

Diana's face was radiating her inner happiness when she hung up the telephone and turned to the waiting Lije. "We leave on Sunday morning," she announced.

His inscrutable expression made it impossible to judge whether he was pleased by her news. Diana knew she was. With luck, it would mean another day in his company.

"Does that mean you'll be working tomorrow?" he asked as his hand rested on the back of her shoulders and guided her out of the restaurant door.

"Not until late tomorrow afternoon, Stella said," Diana answered.

"Have you been to the Alamo or along the river walk?" Lije inquired with that remote indifference that always bewildered her.

"No."

The breeze caught a silver gold lock of hair and blew it across her face. She swept it behind her ear in a graceful gesture as she picked her way among the chunks of gravel in the parking lot.

"I'll conduct you on a personal tour tomorrow."

They had reached the pickup truck as Lije made his statement. It was what she had wanted to hear, but considering his unpredictability she had feared another ambiguous statement. Diana wanted to tell him how much she looked forward to going with him, but all the words that came to mind sounded so trite.

"What time?" she asked as calmly as she could.

"I'll give you a call around nine." His arm was resting on her side of the pickup door, but he was making no attempt to open it. He was looking upward at the night sky brightened with a blanket of stars. "It's a beautiful night, isn't it?"

Diana had been studying his lean angular jaw and cheek and the deep groove carved from the corner of his nose to the corner of his mouth. Even in the dimness of the purple night she could discern that farseeing quality of his eyes, which always made it seem that he could see beyond the horizon. Any moment now he would look down at her. She forced herself to look up at the twinkling lights in the heavens.

"The Big Dipper really stands out tonight," she said when she felt Lije's movement beside her and sensed his eyes on her. "I never have been able to find the Little Dipper. Where is it?"

"The two stars that form the outer edge of the cup point to the North Star. You have to follow their imaginary line."

As Diana continued to search unsuccessfully, Lije moved closer, bringing his arm around her shoulders so she could sight along it. The sudden contact with his lean hardness brought a weakness to her limbs. Masculine cologne enveloped her with its intoxicating scent as his breath stirred her hair. A tightness clamped on her throat as she fought the disturbance that was taking hold of her.

"I still don't see it." She breathed in deeply to cover her sudden shortness of breath.

She made the mistake of turning as she spoke, and found herself at eye level with his mouth. The soft, sensuous curve of his lower lip had a hypnotic effect on her, and Diana couldn't draw her gaze away from it. A hand touched her cheek, the roughness of its skin rasping in a satisfying caress against hers before the thumb lifted the chin. She barely recognized the burning darkness in his usually remote gray eyes.

Without conscious volition her eyelids fluttered shut as Lije moved closer. The invitation for his kiss was written by her parted, glistening lips. The probing kiss was gently firm as he drew her around into his arms. Her hands rose to rest lightly on the back of his neck where dark curling hair waved over his fingers. Diane was torn by conflicting emotions of tenderness and urgency. Her mouth was moving in a restrained response to his as a rising tide of warmth began spreading over her.

The hands that had been holding her easily in his arms began slow, steady movements that brought her closer to him, and the melting of her soft curves against the firmness of his chest produced a corresponding demand in the fiery touch of his lips. Diana willingly obeyed, surrendering eagerly to the increased ardency of his embrace. There was a tormenting ecstasy in the crushing hold. The blood was pounding through her veins, heightening her senses until she was drowning in this new awareness.

Her fingers twined tighter around his neck as she poised herself on tiptoe to get closer to this tall man who was awakening the sleeping passionate side of her nature. His mouth began a thorough inspection of her face and neck, drawing a whispering gasp of pleasure. Deftly Lije pushed her denim jacket away so that only the thin cotton of her shell top separated the growing heat of their bodies. Then his hands were once more at her hips, pressing her against his thighs and revealing his rising need for her. Again his mouth claimed hers, driving away the last tendrils of resistance.

A sniggering laugh sounded several cars away, followed by a male voice saying in what was a loud aside, ''There's a guy that's got it made for tonight!''

Almost before the man's words were out, Lije was pushing Diana away from him and opening the door of the pickup. His breathing was ragged, but his expression was filled with cold anger. He kept a steadying hand on her, since she was still reeling from the effects of his embrace.

"Get in," he ordered thickly.

Her shaking legs were slow to obey, but with the help of his supporting arm she made it. He wasted no time joining her, slipping behind the wheel and starting the motor immediately. They traveled several blocks in what seemed to Diana a freezing silence before Lije turned to look at her.

"I owe you an apology, Diana, for placing you in a position to be subjected to that kind of remark." His speech was clipped and blunt. His eyes that had held such a burning flame were the color of granite again. "I'll take you back to your hotel."

"It didn't upset me." That was a half-truth. Diana had been humiliated that her wanton actions had been seen by others, but the aching void of her empty arms upset her more. "It probably appeared that way to him," she added, studying the fingers knotted in her lap.

"It was more than that, and we both know it!" Lije growled harshly. Her eyes were wide and shimmering like aquamarines when she met his gaze, and she knew he was right. "That was not a casual kiss in the moonlight."

"Not for me," Diana admitted.

"Or me...which is precisely why I'm taking you back to your hotel," he declared. He braked to a stop in front of the hotel, sitting erectly behind the wheel and turning only his face toward her. It was shadowed by the light flowing in behind him from the street outside the window. "Keep in mind, Diana, that you're leaving on Sunday to go one way and I leave on Monday going another."

Half-blinded by the pain his statement caused about the one thing she had been trying to forget, Diana reached for the door handle, wanting only to run away, but his hand reached out, grasping her wrist so she couldn't leave.

"I've learned quite a bit about you in the past twenty-four hours, Diana," Lije went on quietly. "I know you aren't one of those groupies that hang around the rodeo, and as desirable as you are, I can't treat you like one. If you want to call tomorrow off, I'll understand."

"I don't," Diana answered, keeping her head averted.

His hand took her chin and twisted her face around toward him. He was smiling, not just with his eyes but with his whole face.

"Then that makes us both fools, because I don't want to, either." He leaned over, his mouth brushing hers in a light tender kiss before he settled back on his own side of the truck. "I'll call you tomorrow morning."

"Good night, Lije," Diana beamed, slipping out of the truck and smiling back at him. He nodded. She couldn't see his expression, but she felt sure he was still smiling.

THE TELEPHONE RANG at nine o'clock on the dot the next morning. Diana, who had been pacing back and forth beside it, lifted the receiver before it could ring a second time, ignoring the bubbling laughter from her roommate.

"Good morning," she said cheerfully, her heart pounding against her ribs.

"Good morning," Lije echoed. Diana breathed a silent sigh of relief. He had called!

"I'm dressed and ready. Just name the time," she told him.

"I'm going to be tied up this morning, Diana. A friend and business acquaintance of mine just came into town. I won't be able to keep our date today."

"I see." Diana exhaled slowly, the eagerness dying in her voice.

"No, you don't see." Lije mocked her resigned voice. "It's not an excuse. As a matter of fact, I want you to join us for lunch here at the hotel. Will you?"

"Yes," she murmured breathlessly, feeling like a condemned woman who had just been granted a reprieve.

"I'll meet you in the lobby at twelve-thirty."

"I'll be there," she assured him.

There was only one dress in her suitcase, a straight nylon-blend shift with long sleeves. The paisley design of dark blue and red orange made a striking combination with the silver blond of her hair, which she wore down and swirling around her neck and shoulders. It took a great deal of will-power not to go down to the lobby until the appointed time, since she was ready nearly an hour early.

When she finally walked out of the elevator into the lobby, Diana saw Lije talking to a tall, dark-haired man with features as forceful as his own. The instant Lije saw her, he excused himself and walked over to greet her. His eyes made a slow sweeping appraisal of her appearance, quickly reflecting approval and admiration. Her chest swelled with pride at the way he took her arm and led her back to the other man.

"Diana, this is Cord Harris," Lije introduced them. "He owns a ranch over near McCloud, Texas. Cord, this is Diana Mills."

The man was the same height or taller than Lije. His firm jaw was accented by high cheekbones and eyes that matched the color of his hair. There was a smile of approval in his gaze as he shook her hand and glanced briefly at Lije.

"My wife will be joining us shortly," he explained. "Our son required a change of clothes before he was presentable for lunch. She shouldn't be long."

On cue, a woman stepped out of the elevator and walked toward them carrying a dark-haired and dark-eyed one-year-old. The little boy let out a squeal and held out his hands for his father, who gathered him into his arms with a goodly amount of parental pride. There was a loving exchange of glances between the husband and wife that brought a twinge of envy to Diana. Unconsciously her eyes sought Lije at the same moment that he looked at her. There was a flicker of unrest in the gray depths before he turned away.

"This is my wife, Stacy, and our son, Joshua," Cord introduced Diana to his family.

An open, friendly smile brought a pair of dimples into view as Stacy offered her hand to Diana. Shining chestnut gold hair cascaded down the front of an olive green suit that reflected the flecks of green in the warm hazel eyes. Diana liked her immediately and she sensed Stacy's reciprocation. Then Lije was at her side, guiding her into the restaurant.

The men dominated the conversation at the table, but Diana didn't mind. She was able to glean from their talk that Cord Harris raised quarter horses on his ranch and that he was interested in breeding some of his mares with Lije's stallion. Diana assumed he meant the bay Lije used in the steer wrestling until Cord referred to Red as an excellent example of the stallion's potency.

"You wouldn't consider selling Malpais?" Cord asked, expecting the negative answer he received from Lije.

"No, he's part of the future of my ranch," Lije assured him firmly. "I have a couple of his yearlings and two-year-olds that I'd part with, but not Malpais."

"I'd like to look them over." Cord stated.

"Just contact Jim."

"I'll do that."

"These ranchers will talk cattle and horses all day long and into the night." Stacy turned an indulgent smile on her husband.

"It's more interesting than discussing clothes, hairstyles and babies," he mocked her in return.

"If those are your interests, Stacy," Lije joined in, "you and Diana will have a lot in common. She's a model."

"Which hardly qualifies me as an expert," Diana laughed, but she was immediately drawn by Stacy into a conversation that dissipated the last of her reticence.

Three-quarters of an hour later Lije and Cord rose from the table. Cord leaned down and brushed his wife's cheek with a kiss and rumpled his son's dark hair. Diana glanced hesitantly at Lije, wishing she could arouse the look of adoration that had been in Cord's eyes for his wife. A crinkling smile made lines at the corner of the gray eyes.

"I'll see you tonight at the rodeo," said Lije. It should have been a question, but he made it sound like an order.

"I'll be there," Diana answered warmly. His hand touched her shoulder as he passed her chair, following Cord out of the restaurant.

"The three of you make a very handsome family," Diana commented with a trace of envy to the brown-haired girl who was about the same age as she was.

"We're unbelievably happy," Stacy sighed, gazing in the direction her husband had just taken. "I was only half a person until I met Cord."

"How did you meet?" Diana asked. "You don't really have a southern drawl or a Texas twang."

"I'm from the East, New York," Stacy laughed. "I came west after my father died and rented a cabin on Cord's ranch. For a while it was 'east is east and west is west and never the twain shall meet.' We had a very stormy courtship. But all's well that ends well. How long have you known Lije?"

"Not long."

"I only met him myself last year at Cord's annual quarter horse sale. He bought three of our brood mares. Of course, Cord has known him for several years. In some ways Lije reminds me a great deal of Cord. They're both proud, strong men who very capably shape their own destiny." Stacy glanced quizzically at Diana's silent figure. "Before, I've always had the impression that Lije was rather cold and remote, like an eagle circling high in the sky looking on life from afar, but today there was more warmth to him. Because of you?"

"I don't think so."

"Are you in love with him?" Stacy probed gently.

Diana glanced at her sharply, her blue eyes guarded so that they wouldn't reveal how many times in the last twelve hours she had asked herself the same question.

"I know the symptoms," Stacy continued, taking Joshua out of his high chair and wiping his mouth. "It's easier to recognize them in a stranger than it is in yourself. I like Lije and I like you. I couldn't think of a better wish than for the two of you to find the same deep, fulfilling love that Cord and I did."

"You almost make me think it's possible." Diana sighed.

"Anything is possible, Diana, if your love is strong enough," Stacy assured her. Her hazel eyes twinkled merrily. "There is one piece of advice I'd like to give. Neither Cord nor I guessed that the other felt the same way. We almost parted because of it. Don't be afraid to tell him you love him if you do." Stacy paused, her expression growing more solemn.

"I'll try to remember that."

"Gracious!" Stacy exclaimed with a beaming smile. "How did we ever get so serious all of a sudden? Tell me about your work. It must be really interesting being a model. My father was a photographer."

And the subject of Lije Masters was left behind.

CHAPTER FIVE

DIANA LEANED on the stable door. The last wave of nausea was subsiding, leaving her legs trembling and unsteady. The vivid picture of Lije being tossed from the bull and under its hooves was still firmly implanted in her mind's eye. She had stayed in the stands long enough to see him get to his feet completely unharmed before she fled from the arena to the stables.

The clip-clop of a horse's hooves sounded behind her and Diana knew without turning that it was Lije. All the nagging doubts that she really loved him had vanished in those fleeting seconds when he had been in danger. She could feel his eyes resting on her. Squaring her shoulders, she turned to face him. He studied her thoroughly, taking in the pallor in her fair complexion and the fear that still shadowed her eyes. She was looking at his white shirt stained with dirt from the arena floor.

"I don't make a very good rodeo fan," she laughed nervously. "My heart is in my throat too often. Are you all right?"

"A few bruises and pulled muscles." Lije dismounted and led the horse into the stall. "It's all a part of rodeo."

"Like Lefty's broken arms," Diana concluded for him. "Have you ever been hurt seriously?"

"Cracked some ribs a couple of times. I broke my wrist once," He unsaddled the bay and carried the saddle to its rack. His hand came up and touched the bump on his nose. "I broke this once, too. But on the whole I've been lucky."

Diana shuddered, visualizing the horror of seeing Lije being carried from the arena on a stretcher. "I couldn't shrug it off that easily," she said. "I'm not that brave."

"You didn't panic until after it was over, I noticed," Lije smiled. "I saw you in the stands when I stood up. You were afraid, but you waited until you found out I was all right before you collapsed. Bravery is fighting back fear until there isn't any more reason to be afraid. You did fine, Diana."

There was comfort in his words even if she didn't look at it the same way he did. She had been terrified. Her whole world had been on the verge of collapsing.

"Don't think about it anymore," he ordered grimly, his gaze seeing through her mask of composure. "You'll only make it seem all out of proportion."

"I know you're right," she agreed weakly.

"While I'm brushing down Red, you look out at those stars and see if you can find the Little Dipper without me there to distract you," Lije mocked, changing his tactics and winking at her.

It had the desired effect of changing her thoughts to the night before when the stars had

brought her into his arms. The night was decep-
tively clear, making the stars appear to be so close
that she could reach out and touch them. The cold
spell was over and the air was pleasantly warm.
After Lije's teasing and affectionate words, it was
easy for Diana to give herself up to the magic of
the evening. When Lije finished grooming the
horses, she was even able to point with pride to the
Little Dipper with its brilliant North Star.

"I'll have you navigating by the stars in no
time," Lije laughed, pulling her down onto a bale
of hay next to the stable door. "Have you ever
slept outside underneath the stars? Jim and I used
to do it every summer, except when it rained." He
was leaning back against the building, gazing out
into the night. Diana leaned back, too, but she was
covertly studying the faraway expression on his
face. Contentment was blended with a hint of wist-
fulness. "I miss the scent of pine that was always
in the wind at the ranch. And the taste of piñon
nuts that Jim and I used to spend hours gathering."

"It all sounds like a new world to me," Diana
mused.

"A ranch isn't without dangers, too. There's
always rattlesnakes, the odd mountain lion, the
risk of getting lost if you don't know the area, or
thrown from your horse and injured."

"At least you don't invite injury like you do in
the rodeo," Diana answered defiantly, but Lije
just chuckled.

"I'm very careful." His arm curled around her

shoulders and drew her against his chest. She snuggled comfortably against him, relaxing under the soothing caress of his hand in the silken fineness of her hair.

"How did your meeting go with Cord?" she murmured.

"I think he'll probably buy a couple of yearling fillies I have," Lije answered softly. "That will really help, along with the stud fees to service four of his mares. I have a Hereford bull all picked out to improve the bloodline of my cattle. With Cord's money and what I've earned so far this season, it will just about cover the cost of him."

"What else do you want to do with the ranch?"

"Well, I need another couple of wells sunk for water, a new tractor and a stacker for the hay. The list is endless." His lips brushed her forehead and Diana made a little moan of pleasure as she lifted he face for his kiss. It was tender and controlled, but still satisfying. Lije shifted her in his arms and her eyes caught a wince of pain on his face.

"You're hurt!" she accused him, pulling herself out of his arms.

"It's nothing that a little liniment wouldn't cure," he responded, smiling and shaking his head at her disbelieving look. "My muscles are just stiffening up a bit."

"It won't get any better if you don't do something about it." The tone of authority in her voice amused him, but she refused to let the mockery in his eyes deter her.

"Come on." Lije took her hand and pulled her

to her feet. "It might be a welcome change to have someone other than Lefty rub my back and shoulders!"

Blithely Diana followed him to the pickup camper. The efficiently compact interior was amazingly tidy considering the accepted opinion of a bachelor establishment. Lije's tall frame seemed to barely fit in the close quarters. Diana glanced hesitantly around her, wondering where he found room to stretch out.

"The liniment is in the top right-hand cupboard," Lije told her as he unbuttoned his shirt and pulled its tails out of his tan denim Levi's.

Diana averted her head quickly. The sight of the tanned chest with its cloud of dark curling hair had a very unsettling effect on her equilibrium. The bottle of liniment was sitting at the front of the cupboard. Ignoring the rapid beat of her heart, she turned around and opened the bottle with an air of calm briskness.

"Whew!" she exclaimed as the strong scent of the lotion seemed to explode in the air. "This smells terrible!"

"It isn't used as a cologne," Lije chuckled, turning his back to her and sitting crosswise on the couch that did double service as a chair for the small table.

The broad lean back mocked her hesitancy at touching the sinewy ripple of muscles. Resolutely Diana stepped forward, pouring the lotion on her hand. The odor acted as smelling salts, driving away her jittery nerves. There was still something remarkably sensuous about massaging the smooth tanned skin of his back.

"You're very good," Lije observed after several minutes had passed in silence. "Do you do this often?"

"No," she answered, glad his face was turned so he couldn't see the pink in her cheeks. "I just imagine what would feel good if someone were rubbing my back and do that."

Her hands and arms were beginning to ache, but she was enjoying this unrestricted touching of his skin. It was an intimacy that she wanted to prolong. But Lije moved away.

"Any more of that and I'll fall asleep," he said taking her hands and holding them between his own.

"Are you still sore?" she asked.

The old breathlessness had attacked her voice as she stared down at his strong face and the bared chest. He shook his head at her slowly, his gaze straying to her trembling lips. Slowly he pulled her down onto his lap. His fingers captured a lock of her hair that had fallen across her cheek.

"You're very beautiful, Diana," he said huskily.

"I'm glad you think so, Lije," she breathed as his mouth moved closer to hers.

It was a soft, persuasive kiss, not matching the ardor of last night. Yet its very gentleness and tenderness were oddly more satisfying and more sincere. It had the taste of honey and all the sweet things in life. Another dimension of her emotion opened up as Diana discovered a different facet to her love for him. The golden tan of his skin beneath her fingers was more precious than any metal or material wealth.

Lije gently held her away from him, his gray eyes holding the same reflection of mystery and awe that hers did. A furrow cut across his brow and his eyes narrowed. When he cupped his hand behind her neck and drew her to him, he kissed her with savagery and hunger. The ruthless barbarism was equally potent. The iron bands of his arms held her so tightly she could barely breathe while twin hearts hammered as one.

Then his hands were digging into the flesh of her arms as he firmly set her back on her feet. He raked his fingers through his wavy chestnut hair and rose to his feet, pushing past her to yank a shirt out of the small closet. Diana waited. Lije was in charge. She would do whatever he wanted.

"Wait outside for me," he ordered crisply. "I think it's time we went for our coffee."

Diana meekly obeyed and Lije followed almost immediately, taking time only to comb his rumpled hair into order and button his shirt. The café they had stopped at the first night was closed. It was after midnight, the witching hour. Lije turned the truck in the direction of her hotel.

"It's just as well," he said grimly. The gray eyes were uncompromising as he glanced over at her. "We would only be prolonging the inevitable."

Diana swallowed as tears burned the back of her eyes. All evening she had been avoiding facing the fact that this was their last night. The bliss-filled moments with Lije had succeeded in wiping it from her mind until now.

"When will you be in Houston? I thought I'd drive down to see you." It was hard forcing those casual words through the lump in her throat.

"Have you forgotten so soon the agony you went through tonight?" Lije sneered. "How much more hell do you want to put yourself through? It will be the same every time I get into the arena."

Unable to answer his knife-sharp questions, Diana blinked unseeingly at the lights of the hotel shining ahead of them. She still couldn't speak when he parked in front of it and sat silently behind the wheel.

"It has to be goodbye, Diana."

Her chin quivered, but she firmly raised it from her chest. "Maybe I'll see you in Dallas?" She smiled brightly.

"I won't be going there this year." he told her. His coldness made it clear that he was severing their relationship completely. In one quick movement he reached across her and opened the door. "Goodbye, Diana."

"Goodbye," she answered in a choked voice as she scrambled out of the truck. Before she had time to turn around, Lije was driving away.

DIANA DIDN'T SLEEP that night. Nor did she toss and turn in the bed. Her frozen body was immobile, as were the tears in her eyes. Lije liked her. He cared for her, but not to the extent that she

cared for him. Otherwise he couldn't have shoved
her out of his life. But where had her tenacity
been? Fate had denied her many things—parents;
a home, childhood memories of family love. Was
fate denying her the man she loved, as well? Or
had she grown so used to accepting the cruel blows
of life that she had no strength of will to fight?

Not until Stella called her did Diana open the
eyes that had been feigning sleep. She went
through the motions of packing, her continued
silence drawing curious looks from the other girl.

"Is your cowboy coming this morning to say
goodbye?" Stella asked.

"I don't know," Diana replied with studied indifference, but it was the wish foremost in her
mind to see him just once more.

But as she stood in the lobby with Stella waiting
for Rick to bring the station wagon around to the
front, Diana knew Lije wouldn't come. Her suitcases and cosmetic bag were in her hands. In
another few minutes she would be on her way to
Dallas. Stacy Harris's words came drifting back to
Diana. "Don't be afraid to tell him you love him."

"Bring your bags. We're ready to go," Connie
ordered, walking into the lobby and waving toward Stella and Diana.

Together Diana and Stella walked out the door.
Rick took the suitcases from Stella and loaded
them in the rear of the wagon. Just ahead of the
car was a taxi cab. As Rick walked back to take
Diana's things, she stepped away from him.

"I'm not going," she said unblinkingly.

"What do you mean?" Connie demanded, but Diana was already hurrying toward the vacant taxi.

Her mind was made up. She was going to the rodeo grounds. She was going to find Lije and tell him that she was in love with him. If. . .if it didn't matter to him, then—well, she'd decide what to do then.

The first place she went after the taxi dropped her off was to the stables. The buckskin was in his stall, but the red bay was gone and so was Lije. Diana paused to steady her trembling legs, then proceeded toward the arena. He was there, standing next to a group of cowboys, his back to her as he tightened the cinch to his saddle. She walked slowly toward him, the big horse blocking her from the view of the other cowboys.

"Hey, Lije!" one of them called. "You gonna see that pretty blond again tonight?"

"No!" Lije answered sharply, giving a vicious tug on the cinch and causing the horse to move nervously.

"I'd be more than glad to stand in for you," another man replied, drawing sniggering laughs from the rest of the group.

"Shut up, Rafe." Lije's order carried an ominous threat in its softly spoken words.

"He's been like that all morning." Diana recognized Lefty Robbins's voice. "That little blond put a burr under his saddle, I think."

"That's enough out of you, too, Lefty." Lije gathered the reins and turned to lead the horse away. As he turned, he came face to face with Diana. His head came up slowly as the arrogant gray eyes surveyed her.

"Hello, Lije," she murmured. Her movement was frozen by the coldness in his gaze.

"What are you doing here?" he demanded. "You should be halfway to Dallas by now."

"I couldn't leave." Diana swallowed, feeling her courage fast deserting her. She inhaled deeply. "I'm in love with you, Lije."

He took a step toward her, then another. His eyes were dark fires smoldering with what Diana mistook for anger.

"I didn't mean to, Lije," she hurried her words. "It just happened. Love isn't something you can turn on and off at will."

Her eyes pleaded up at him to understand, to stop looking so arrogantly down at her. His hands reached out and dug into the flesh of her shoulders. Diana steeled herself to endure the shaking that was coming, but instead, Lije lifted her into the air above his head, then slowly lowered her to eye level. With her feet still dangling off the ground, he proceeded to kiss her. He kissed her so thoroughly that when he lowered her to the ground amid the scattering of applause from the onlooking cowboys Diana could barely stand on her shaking legs.

"Let's get out of here," he muttered, picking up her cases, which had at some time tumbled to the ground.

"Lije?"

Her hand touched his arm and he smiled down at her. It was a miracle. That was love shining out of his eyes. An arm swept around her waist as he hustled her out of the arena.

Lije didn't stop until they reached his pickup camper, then only long enough to open the door and push Diana inside. She would have gone back into his arms then, but he held her at arm's length.

"We have to talk first, Diana," he said firmly. "And I can't think straight when I hold you."

"There's nothing to talk about." Diana smiled, supremely confident in the face of his love for her. "I'll follow you all over the country or all over the world."

"No. I meant what I said last night. I couldn't put you through the agony of wondering every time I was in the arena whether I was going to come out in one piece."

"Then I'll wait for you. Two years, three years, whatever it takes."

"I can't wait that long for you." There was no mistaking the reason for the burning look in his eyes.

"I'm in love with you, Lije. I can't let you go." Panic crept into her voice and involuntarily she moved closer to him.

"There is an alternative," he said, gripping her shoulders to halt her movement. "But it won't be easy. I can quit the rodeo and go back to the ranch. It will mean some lean years where we'll have to do without a lot of things, but we could make it."

"You said you needed another two years at least," she murmured. "How can you do it?"

"I can sell Red," Lije sighed grudgingly. "I had hoped to keep him for a second stallion. As it is I'll only get half what he's worth, but it will give me the money to make the necessary improvements to the ranch to get us by for a couple of years."

"I could keep on working, Lije," Diana offered. Her heart went out to him because of the sacrifice he was making for her. "I have a little money saved now. Not much really, but—"

"No! Absolutely not!" he barked. "Listen, darling," he went on more calmly. "I'm the original male chauvinist, but my wife is going to be with me wherever I am, not off posing for some guy with a camera. We'll make it together."

"That's the way I want it, too," she whispered earnestly.

"I love you, Diana." The hands that had held her away now drew her to him as Lije proceeded to rain kisses on her lips, nose, eyes, and neck. "Tonight will be my last rodeo, darling," he murmured against her cheek. "Tomorrow we'll drive to El Paso. We can get married in Juarez, Mexico. By Tuesday, we'll be at my ranch...our ranch... our home. Is that too long to wait?"

"I would wait a lifetime if you wanted me to," Diana breathed, her happiness knowing no limits when he held her like this in his arms. His mouth covered hers quickly, letting her know without words that that wasn't necessary.

With a shaky laugh of exaltation Lije lifted his

head from hers. "The first thing we'd better do is get you checked back into a hotel for tonight."

"Do I have to?" she asked impishly.

"Yes," he growled mockingly. "This afternoon you can go out and buy yourself a wedding dress while I handle a few other things."

"You're the boss!" Her blue eyes twinkled up at him demurely. She was rewarded for her meek acceptance with another kiss and a promise of more.

CHAPTER SIX

"WELL, MRS. MASTERS?" Lije looked at her lovingly. "You're now in New Mexico, the land of enchantment. Are you happy?"

"Very happy," she answered, snuggling closer to him as she gazed out the window of the pickup truck at the thinning marks of civilization.

It was all too wonderful to believe it had happened, Diana thought, sneaking a glance at the man who, last night, had become her husband in every sense of the word. She still marveled at how tender and gentle he had been with her when he had discovered that she had never been with a man before. And she had been astounded by her own response. Lije had always been able to arouse her, but Diana had never believed that she could be transported to that level of rapture.

"Darling, are you sure you don't mind not having a honeymoon? We could spare a few days in El Paso. We aren't that far away that we couldn't turn back." The concern and desire to please in Lije's gaze made Diana's heart leap with love.

"I'd rather go home, Lije," she assured him.

"I hope you won't be disappointed," he said quietly. "Don't conjure up images of an enormous house with plush furnishings. It's just a one-story frame house that's seen better days. Someday I'll build a new home for you, but—"

Diana placed her hand on his mouth to hush his proud apologies. "If you're there, it will seem like a palace to me."

His arm circled her shoulders and pulled her closer against his chest while he drove with one hand on the wheel.

"With you, right now I feel like a king," he assured her, taking his attention from the four-lane highway long enough to give her a quick kiss. "There are so many places I want to show you. Where I used to hunt when I was a kid. We'll sleep out under the stars sometimes, too, when it's warmer. I hope you grow to love the ranch as much as I do, Diana."

"I will."

When they turned west out of Socorro and left the Rio Grande Valley behind, the landscape began to change. The few towns they passed were minuscule compared to the metropolis of Dallas/ Fort Worth where Diana had lived all her life. The mountains, too, seemed more rugged and forbidding, even with their pine-covered slopes. Diana was beginning to realize what an alien world she was coming to live in.

She wouldn't let the distances daunt her, not even when Lije turned off the main road onto a dirt one and several miles later turned off of it onto a two-rutted track that led off into the mountains.

"This is the ranch," he announced. His gray eyes left the land around them to look at his wife. There was so much pride and contentment in his gaze that Diana had to smile.

"It's like something out of a Western movie."

There was not a cloud in the azure blue sky or a telltale mark of civilization to blot its horizon. Snow-capped mountain peaks sloped away to plateaus, mesas and rolling plains where patches of snow melted slowly in the shadowed areas of grass. The rutted track stretched endlessly into these hills without a sign of any buildings. The emptiness, isolation, the immense space all struck Diana simultaneously. Gone was the security of tall skyscrapers and crowds of people that had constituted her life. Lije had told her that his ranch was miles from anywhere, but the force of his statement didn't sink in until now.

At last they topped a rise and the buildings of the ranch were ahead of them. As they drew closer, Diana could see a weathered one-story house standing away from the outbuildings. The fact that it had more windows than the others was the only difference between them. All the buildings were a dirty white, their paint chipped and peeling.

"The first trip into town I'll buy some paint," Lije said grimly. "I assure you the framework is sound and sturdy."

"Don't do it for my sake," Diana said quickly, glancing up to meet the masked expression on his face, wondering if her disappointment had shown on her face. "If you need the money for something else, don't worry about making an impression on me."

"The money will stretch to cover paint. Just because the ranch isn't as prosperous as it could be is no reason that it can't look that way." Lije smiled down at her, removing his arm from around her and gradually slowing the pickup down to a halt near the first of the buildings. "I'll put Buck away. then we'll go up to the house together."

Diana slid out of the pickup after Lije, following him to the rear where the horse trailer was hitched. This was a homecoming for her husband—she could tell by the light glowing in his eyes when he looked at the corral and the horses inside. They were his. Everything on the place belonged to him and the pride of ownership was in his face. But Diana felt out of place, a stowaway who had no business here at all. She touched her gold wedding band to reassure herself. Lije had enough to worry about without bringing up her insecure feelings. She had always been able to adjust to anything. And now, as his wife, she had even more reason.

The breeze was cool, carrying the sting of biting cold from the mountaintops. Diana drew her blue corduroy parka closer around her neck as she followed Lije to the corral. While he was engaged in caring for the horse, she took the opportunity to study the ranch yard, determined to become familiar with everything. A movement was detected out of the corner of her eye and she turned to look. A man was walking out of a nearby building. He had jet black hair that hung over his forehead and his cheekbones were wide and prominent, setting off the deep-sunk dark eyes. He, too, had on a heavy parka jacket over faded blue Levi's. At first she thought he was of Mexican descent, but as he came closer Diana could tell he was an Indian.

"Lije?" Her voice was raised with a trace of questioning fear. She glanced at her husband.

Lije was just shutting the corral gate when she called to him. Following the direction of her gaze, which she had returned to the strange man still walking closer, his firm stride quickly carried him past Diana toward the man. She braced herself, expecting to see Lije order the man off the property, then stared in stunned disbelief as he clasped the stranger's hand in both of his and shook it warmly. Lije's broad back blocked out the man's face, but the friendly tone of their voices reaffirmed the handshake.

"Diana, come here," Lije called, a grin spreading across his face. She was glad of his arm around her waist when she reached his side. "I want you to meet Jim Two Pony, my friend and my foreman."

"How do you do?" Diana nodded nervously.

There was no welcoming light in the dark eyes that looked back at her, only taciturn reserve. The barest inclination of his head indicated that Jim Two Pony had heard her words before he turned back to Lije.

"It is good to have you back, Lije," the man said in a bland but well-educated voice.

"I didn't expect you to be here at the house

when we arrived." Lije smiled, taking no notice of Jim's lack of attention to Diana. "I thought I'd have to go into the mountains to find you."

"The jeep broke down again. I was fixing it," Jim replied. His mouth moved and the words came out, but there was never any discernible change in his expression.

"I'll take Diana up to the house, then I'll come down and give you a hand. It's good to be back, Jim." Lije clasped the man's shoulder for a brief moment before he turned to Diana. "I might as well start to work right away," he said to her.

"Of course," she agreed. She had to force herself to smile. If Jim Two Pony had wanted to make her feel more of an outsider, then he had succeeded.

"Hey, you're awfully quiet." As they reached the house Lije lifted her chin and warmed her lips with a kiss. "I think it's time for the groom to carry the bride over the threshold."

He opened the door leading into the house, then turned to Diana. The coldness that had begun to numb her swiftly fled away under the adoring look in his gray eyes.

"I love you, Lije," she whispered fervently as he swept her up into his arms.

"You'd better, Mrs. Masters," he grinned, walking through the door with Diana's arms firmly entwined around his neck.

She clung tightly to his hand as he set her feet down on the yellow linoleum floor of the kitchen. She glanced around at the old-fashioned white metal cabinets and the heavy porcelain sink. A square wooden table and chairs sat in the middle of the room. The white paint that covered them had turned a dingy yellow. Against the sidewall was an electric stove of antique vintage. Faded curtains of drab yellow hung at the window above the sink and the one near the cabinets. The walls were covered with old-fashioned glaze paper with a nondescript design of yellow flowers.

"None of the house has a decorator's touch, but it's serviceable. It needs a woman's touch, Diana. Yours," Lije told her with a loving glance at her silver blond head. "Let me show you the rest of the house."

The living room was roomy, but with the same austere look that would be expected with only masculine inhabitants. A fireplace was on the outside wall, its hearth blackened from its many fires. There was a little nook that had been intended as a formal dining area. Lije had installed a desk and office files to maintain the records for the ranch. A small bedroom was opposite the larger main bedroom. Both were sparsely furnished with little decoration to relieve the effect of the heavy furniture. The bathroom was large, with an old bathtub that was supported by cast-iron legs.

Nothing in the house remotely resembled the bright and cheery apartment complete with all the modern conveniences that Diana had lived in these last few years. She tried hard not to let her dislike of the bare and drab house show. After all, it was Lije's home, and his running commentary revealed the warm and loving memories he associated with it. It wasn't his fault that he didn't see it with a stranger's eyes. Diana was the first one to agree that beautiful furnishings did not make a house into a home.

"I know you'll want to unpack and prowl around the house on your own," said Lije, leading her again into the kitchen.

"Yes, I'd like that," Diana agreed quietly. She walked to the window over the sink and gazed out. From there she could barely make out the figure of Jim Two Pony working in the shadow of one of the buildings. "Why didn't you ever mention that Jim was an Indian?"

She heard his footsteps bringing him closer to her. "I thought I had. Does it make any difference?"

There was something very cold about his question. Diana turned around, staring up into the suddenly remote expression. She knew immediately that she had said the wrong thing.

"No, not at all." She looked back at the window, her fingers clenching the cold porcelain sink. "I just never knew any Indians before. He startled me." She laughed a nervous tight laugh. Was she prejudiced because Jim Two Pony was an Indian? She didn't think so. Yet why had she assumed that Lije would throw him off the property? "I felt awkward and uneasy."

"Jim is a full-blooded Navaho. They're a very proud race. A stranger often receives the impression that he's being regarded with a bit of superiority by a Navaho," Lije explained. "They have hearts just like you and I, and they feel things just as intensely as we do. They just don't show it as readily."

"The Navahos were a peaceful tribe, weren't they?"

"In some ways. But I think it was more a case of being realistic. The white man seemed to be without numbers. Fighting would have been futile if they wanted to preserve their race, so the Navaho chose to adapt before their tribe was reduced to the point that it would die. Don't let that mislead you into thinking they were not strong and powerful. The Apache, who were notorious warriors, raided other Indian tribes as well as white settlements, but they usually avoided attacking the Navaho. They knew the Navaho's retribution would be swift and sure."

"You admire them, don't you?" Diana asked. Her back was still to him so he couldn't see her expression filled with love for this compassionate, understanding man she had married.

"Yes," Lije said simply. "Jim is my friend, the closest thing to a brother I'll ever have. I can't expect you to feel the same way I do toward him. But don't stereotype him as a worthless bum and look down on him as an object of pity."

"I don't!" Diana whirled around sharply, stung by the cold, contemptuous anger in his voice. The beginnings of retaliatory anger rose in her only to be restrained quickly. "Oh, darling, maybe at first I thought of him that way. But it was only from ignorance and never being exposed to Indians before. I honestly hold nothing against Jim. Wherever you are, I will be; and your friends are mine. Don't let's quarrel the first day in our new home."

He studied her quietly for a minute before he drew her into his arms and held her close against his chest. "Forgive me, Diana," he murmured into her hair. "It's just that I've seen the contempt that comes into some people's eyes when they see an Indian. I should have realized that you were too sensitive to be blinded by a man's race."

"I'm human." Diana tilted her head back to gaze up at him. "Perhaps I was blinded for a moment, but only for a moment."

Lije gave her a long, slow kiss that left her clinging to him weakly. "I'll stay here all day if you keep reacting like that," he teased.

She snuggled under his chin, enjoying the feeling of his warm body next to hers and the wayward movements of his hands on her body.

"Promises, promises, that's all I ever get," she murmured, smiling up at the passionate gleam in his eyes.

"You just keep that thought in mind." Lije touched the tip of her nose. "And we'll find out how true that is tonight. Right now, Jim is probably wondering where I am."

"He probably knows," Diana laughed, moving out of her husband's arms. "Now run along, so your poor little wife can get something done."

"I have half a mind to stay and teach you who

gives the orders around here." He reached over and swung her playfully back into his arms. "But I'll save that for tonight, too."

"Mmmm, I have a lot to look forward to tonight," she murmured against his lips.

"You make it very hard for a man to leave." This time it was Lije who set her away from him, then walked to the door.

"In case you get tied up with Jim all afternoon, what time is dinner?" Diana asked as he started out the door.

"With all the work I have to do tonight, you'd better make it early, around six," he answered with a decided twinkle in his eye.

"Yes, Mr. Masters." Diana dropped him a little curtsy to accompany her demure words. Lije was smiling as he walked out the door.

Unpacking didn't take long since most of her things were still in Dallas. Diana had written to Stella to send them on. Yet there had been something pleasant and intimate about rearranging the clothes in the chest of drawers to make room for hers. The act of putting her husband's clothes away made their marriage seem more real and not something that had happened in a dream. When she could find nothing else to do in the bedroom, she reluctantly went to the kitchen.

No matter how drab and dreary it looked, it was her kitchen now. She was in charge of the meals and the dishes and everything else. The sooner she became familiar with the location of things, the sooner it, too, would seem as if it belonged to her.

Looking around at its worn funishings, Diana realized that the only thing that would improve the kitchen's appearance was a complete remodeling. The money from Lije's rodeo winnings and the sale of the blood bay horse would certainly never stretch to cover such a luxury. She would just have to suffer with the way it was.

Dinner was on the stove when Lije came in a little before six o'clock. Diana was setting the table with the ironstone plates from the cupboard. Lije planted a kiss on her cheek, then started into the other room to wash up.

"You only need two place settings," he said.

"Isn't Jim eating with us?" Diana held the third plate in her hand.

"Not tonight." Lije's voice carried from the small hallway. "I think he figured we would want to be alone."

"Is that what he said?" she asked.

"Not in so many words."

Unbidden the thought sprung to mind that maybe Jim just didn't want to eat dinner with her, but she quickly banished it. Lije was undoubtedly right, and Jim was just trying to be thoughtful. Still, Diana had received the distinct impression that Jim didn't like her. It was a feeling that wasn't easy to shake. And despite Lije's earlier assumption that it had to do with the difference of their skin, Diana thought it was a case of individual likes and dislikes.

The first meal she had ever cooked for Lije was an unqualified success. He laughingly confided afterward that he hadn't had the nerve to inquire about her cooking abilities.

"Well, for having such doubts about your wife," Diana said with mock anger, "you can help with the dishes!"

It was an idyllic evening, just the way Diana had always pictured it to be. Later, after Lije had good-naturedly helped with the dishes, they had gone into the living room where Lije built a fire in the darkened fireplace. The cheery flames had brought an added spark into the room, chasing away some of its gloom. They had sat on the camelbacked brown tweed sofa comfortably wrapped in each other's arms. From some distant place in the outdoors a howling sound penetrated the walls of the house. Its wailing sound made Diana shudder and curl tighter against the broad chest.

"What was that? A wolf?" she asked, glancing at the windows, which only reflected the light from the room.

"Coyotes," Lije answered grimly.

"They aren't dangerous, are they?" she breathed more confidently.

"They aren't unless you're a sheep or a lamb." Lije moved restlessly, finally rising to poke the fire again.

"Are you worried about your flocks?"

"Yes." Lije sighed heavily. "We've lost more lambs than I'd like to count to coyotes."

"Who takes care of your sheep?"

"I have a sheepherder and his dogs with each

flock. They travel around in a wagon quite similar in appearance in some ways to the Conestoga wagons that brought the settlers west.''

"Don't they protect the sheep from the coyotes?"

Another yelping howl drifted eerily into the room, answered by an echoing call. It was another vivid reminder that Diana's alien world was just outside, regardless of how content she had been in Lije's arms.

"They do the best they can, but coyotes are very bold. Mountain lions flee to the mountains and the more remote regions when man moves onto the land. The coyote doesn't have that fear of man. He treats us with healthy respect, but he keeps hanging around and becoming more of a menace than a nuisance. Especially to ranchers." Lije turned away from the fire to smile at Diana. "Now how did we get on this subject?"

"The coyotes were howling outside."

Lije walked back to the couch. "It's time we forgot about what's outside," he said huskily, bending over Diana and propelling her back against the cushions.

CHAPTER SEVEN

DIANA FELT LIJE nuzzling her ear and she turned sleepily over for his kiss. Bright sunlight tried hard to penetrate her closed eyelids. His mouth was warm and moist against hers.

"Good morning, sleeping beauty," he whispered. "It's time to get up."

Diana moaned, slowly blinking her eyes while she focused on the man sitting beside her. He was wearing a plaid shirt of yellow and dark blue with a pair of worn Levi's. Then she noticed the cup of coffee in his hand.

"I brought you some coffee," he said, handing it to her as she plumped the pillow behind her and pulled herself into a sitting position.

"You're already dressed," she murmured. "What time is it?"

"Nearly seven. I've already been up for a couple of hours, but I thought I'd let you sleep this morning." Lije smiled.

"You shouldn't have done that. Let me get up and fix your breakfast." She took a quick sip of her coffee as she started to pull back the bedclothes.

"Too late—I've already eaten. But I left the

dishes in the sink for you." He kissed her again and let his mouth trail along her neck.

"Thanks a lot," she gasped as his caress raised havoc with her heartbeat.

"I'll be out with the horses this morning, but this afternoon we're going into town to pick up supplies. Make a list of the things you'll need." After bringing her hands to his mouth, Lije rose from the bed.

After finishing the luncheon dishes, Diana and Lije left for town. He dropped her off at the grocery store with the daunting reminder to buy enough to last two weeks, when they would make another trip into town. For Diana that was a tall order, since she had no idea what her husband's likes and dislikes were and only a rough idea of his appetite. About Jim Two Pony she knew nothing.

Lije had told her where he would be parking his truck and that when she was done he would meet her at a local restaurant. He was sitting at a table when she walked in. Rising, he held out the adjoining chair for her.

"Are you all done?" he asked, signaling the waitress for a cup of coffee for Diana.

"I hope so," Diana sighed, shrugging off her parka. "I've got that terrible feeling that I've forgotten something important."

The restaurant door opened and a young girl in pigtails walked in, slender and boyishly attractive in tight blue Levi's and denim parka. Something in her naturally buoyant movement attracted Diana's attention. The girl's bright questioning eyes roamed over the room, coming to light on their table.

"Lije? Lije Masters!" The girl hurried gaily toward them, cowboy boots clicking loudly on the floor. "You're supposed to be in Houston! What are you doing here?"

As the girl reached their table, Lije rose to his feet and the girl threw her arms around his neck and kissed him soundly on the cheek. Diana watched in stunned silence. The girl had taken no appreciable notice of her.

"What are you doing here, Patty?" Lije asked, calmly removing her hands from around his neck and offering her a chair at their table.

"Libby was a little off-color when the tour started. I came back to pick him up for the Houston rodeo." Pert brown eyes turned on Diana. "Hi, I'm Patty King."

"This is my wife, Diana," Lije inserted before Diana had a chance to reply. "Patty is a trick rider in the rodeo. And Libby is one of her horses."

"Your wife?" Diana noticed the flicker of pain show just for a moment in the brown eyes before it was quickly concealed. A provocatively playful look was darted at Lije. "I let you out of my sight for two weeks and you get yourself married!" Patty declared, turning to Diana with an impish smile on her face. "You just can't trust a man for a moment! But anyway, congratulations to both of you."

"Thank you," Diana smiled. Although it was obvious to her that Patty was in love with Lije, she couldn't help liking her. The youthful openness was both charming and appealing.

Patty turned to Lije. "You still haven't told me why you aren't in Houston. Have you left the rodeo?"

"For good." Lije glanced briefly at Diana, letting Patty know without words the reason. "I sold Red and I'm going back to ranching full time."

"How is Jim? I haven't seen him in ages." Patty changed the subject.

"He has had his hands full, but he's fine," Lije answered.

"Tell him I said hello. Well, I imagine you two newlyweds would rather be alone, and it's time I hit the road." Patty rose to her feet. "It was nice meeting you, Diana. Take good care of Lije. You've got one great guy here. I know."

"She's very nice," Diana commented after the goodbyes had been said and Patty had left.

"There isn't anyone quite like her." Lije agreed. "She always has a smile."

"She's very fond of you." Her probing comment was intended to find out how Lije felt about Patty.

"We've known each other quite a while and we have a lot in common. Are you ready to head back to the ranch?"

That was all she was going to get out of Lije, Diana realized. Patty and Lije probably did have a lot in common, and they had followed the rodeo circuit. She shivered inwardly as she wondered whether things would have turned out the same if Patty had been at the San Antonio rodeo.

HER SECOND DAY at the ranch Diana struggled out of bed before the sun. She didn't function very well the first thing in the morning, and it wasn't even morning yet. Lije exhibited amazing forbearance with her fumbling attempts to be organized and efficient. Streaks of pale light were just beginning to glimmer on the horizon when breakfast had been consumed.

"What are you going to do today?" Diana asked with forced brightness as she poured herself another cup of much-needed coffee.

"I'm going to check the east pasture. The cattle have pretty well grazed out the winter field and they'll have to be moved soon," Lije answered, rising from the table and walking to the small closet just to the left of the door leading outside. "I'll probably be late for lunch, so don't worry about me."

After shrugging into his heavy sheepskin-lined parka, Lije reached back into the closet and withdrew a rifle, its metal barrel gleaming menacingly at Diana.

"Wh-what are you doing with that gun?" she stammered.

"I'm taking it with me." A puzzled light was in the gray eyes as he looked over his shoulder.

"Why? What for?" The paralyzing numbness left her limbs, allowing her to rise from her chair and rush toward him. "Oh, Lije, you don't have to take that gun, do you? I can't stand guns."

"Diana, don't be childish," he admonished her gently as he reached back inside the closet and extracted a box of shells, which he stuffed in his coat pocket.

"What do you need it for?" she persisted, her pale face turned up to him in a more effective plea.

"I always have a rifle in the rack of my pickup when I'm on the ranch." His steadying hand held her shoulder firmly. "There are times when you need it."

"When?" she cried.

"I told you last night that coyotes are a plague. If I see one out there, I don't think he'll wait until I drive all the way back to the ranch to get my rifle and then back." There was a bite of irritation in his voice at her naive, feminine fears, followed by a brisk kiss directed at her cheek. "I have to leave now."

As he donned his cowboy hat and walked out the door, Diana wondered unwillingly whether Patty would have reacted the way she had, then decided that Patty King would probably be the type that could shoot nearly as well as Lije. But logic wouldn't reason away her fear. Diana loathed the violence and killing that were automatically connected with guns. And her husband carried one.

"Don't worry." His words succeeded in doing the opposite. Diana was a nervous wreck before he drove into the yard in the early afternoon. It was all she could do to keep herself from rushing out the door and flinging herself in his arms, but this time she controlled her anxiety and greeted him calmly when he entered the house. Judging by their conversation during lunch, the subject had been forgotten by both.

But the strain and tension didn't ease for Diana. Her senses and emotions during the next days were assaulted by foreign elements. The profound silence of her new world was the first impact. No more blare of horns or screech of tires and loud voices were surrounding her as they had done for so many years. When the silence was broken, it was by alien animal sounds that more often than not sent an eerie chill down her spine.

The days were long and lonely. Lije left the house at sunrise and often didn't return until sundown. Diana tried to fill the empty hours with familiar things. The house was spotless. The furniture gleamed from repeated, unnecessary polishings. All the rooms were permeated with continual baking odors from the kitchen. Nothing she did eliminated the feeling that the house was her island surrounded by an ocean of unending grasslands and distant, scowling mountains.

The qualities that had drawn her to Lije—strength of purpose, arrogant dominance, and driving ambition—were the very things that kept them apart. It wasn't in him to slack if there was work to be done. For Diana, that meant fewer hours spent with her. Not even the evenings were sacred anymore, as Lije spent more and more of that time at the desk in the living-room alcove. As Diana found the adjustment harder and harder to make, Lije thrived on it. He stepped out to meet each challenge head on.

Diana knew how important it was to their future that this year be successful, and she knew that Lije was determined to make it that way for the security of both of them. After putting her foot in her mouth once, expressing her dislike of guns, she could not add to her husband's burden by letting him know that the isolation and strangeness were getting to her. She kept silent about her loneliness, her failure to find any beauty in the harshness of her environment, and the empty feeling that again she didn't belong.

This last feeling was intensified by Jim Two Pony's attitude toward her. He did concede to taking the evening meal with Diana and Lije, but all other meals he had at his small cabin erected in the woods some distance from the rest of the ranch buildings. Never had he directed any conversation toward her and he replied to any of her questions in monosyllables. Diana felt sure that the slight air of remoteness that Lije possessed came from a long association with Jim Two Pony. That knowledge made it a little harder for her to try to reach out to Lije.

After more than three weeks on the ranch with only a second trip into town to break the monotony of her days, the drab walls of the house closed around her like a prison. She had rarely ventured out of the house except to accompany Lije to bid him a last goodbye before he left. As she had never been an outdoor person, the cool mountain breeze had always seemed too brisk for walking. But this afternoon there was no other alternative. There were enough pies, cakes, and cookies in the freezer to last a month. The house was immaculate. She had read and reread the few magazines and books in the house. Her hair was washed. Her nails were polished. And it was barely two o'clock.

With an air of resigned indifference Diana changed into a pair of slacks and sturdy shoes. Minutes later she was buttoning her jacket and stepping out the door. The sun had climbed its blue ladder until it rested nearly overhead, preparing for its downward slide to the west. The breeze was gentle, carrying a wild mingling of smells, from horses to sheep to cattle to the fragrant pines and the scent of hay. But the odors were unfamiliar to Diana and she couldn't pick out one from the other.

The house had no lawn, just a continuance of the yellow grasses that covered the hills. There were no hedges, no flowering bushes, no shade trees except for the pines behind the house and a scrubby-looking pine-type tree in the front. The white paint that Lije had bought to redo the buildings was in the storeroom in the house. There had been too many other things that needed to be done before spring, so the painting had been set aside.

First Diana strolled toward the fenced pasture where some horses had gathered. For a while she leaned against the wooden rails watching the shaggy-coated animals as they quietly grazed. A distant, smaller enclosure held a lone horse that Diana knew from the conversation between Lije and Jim was the stallion Malpais. At this distance he looked solid black in color, although Lije had said he was a bay with black points.

The yearlings in the corral where Diana was became curious about this human who made no move toward them and began moving en masse in her direction. Before they could reach her Diana stepped away. She couldn't treat them like overgrown dogs the way Lije and Jim Two Pony did.

A movement near the barn drew her attention. Jim Two Pony was arranging some gear in the back end of the pickup before walking back into the barn. Diana hesitated. Lije was out somewhere on the range and wouldn't be back until dusk. Here was her opportunity to have a private conversation with this man who seemed to determined to ignore her presence.

Resolutely her feet carried her toward the dark confines of the barn, illuminated only by the sunlight filtering through the dusty windows and the open door. Diana knew that Jim Two Pony had to have heard her steps, but he didn't glance up when her silhouette blocked the doorway.

"Hello, Jim," she said with determined brightness.

"Hello," was his clipped reply as he walked over and took a saddle from its rack near the door.

"Is Lije around?" Diana asked, knowing that if it were up to Jim the conversation had just ended.

"Nope." He walked to the door, the saddle carried effortlessly over his shoulder and Diana following a few steps behind.

"Do you know where he is?" she persisted.

"Nope."

"It's a nice day, isn't it? The sun really feels good." Diana stubbornly refused to give up.

"Yes." Cold, dark eyes flicked over her.

"How much longer before spring comes?" There was the barest glimmer of a twinkle in her eye as she silently dared Jim Two Pony to find a one-word reply to that.

"Soon."

Diana pressed her lips together. "Why don't you like me, Jim?" she asked, hoping her bluntness would shock him into revealing the truth.

"You are very beautiful," he replied without blinking an eye.

"Is that the reason why you don't like me?" Diana asked grimly.

"Beauty is as beauty does." His bland composure wasn't the least bit ruffled.

"What you're really saying is that you don't think I'm right for Lije. That even though we both love each other very much, I don't belong here." She tilted her chin upward, letting the light breeze flow over her face and catch at the silken fineness of her pale hair.

"When I first came to this ranch after Lije's mother died, she had tried to grow roses by the house. They withered away. They could not exist without her pampering and care." The offhand way Jim was talking would have led a stranger to believe he was recounting a story instead of answering Diana's question.

Yet Diana understood his analogy perfectly. She

was the rose who needed special attention from Lije in order to survive. Lije was her only reason for being here. Diana didn't comment. She knew Jim Two Pony was going to continue, despite his previous silences.

"There is a plant that grows wild on the ranch called a yucca. It thrives on this land. Its sword-shaped leaves have fibers that Indians previously used to make cloth and baskets. In the spring its towering center stalk is covered with waxy bell-shaped flowers. This plant contributes more than just beauty. It belongs."

With that cold, unemotional statement, Jim Two Pony walked into the near corral, leaving Diana standing ashen-faced and alone. She had long guessed the way he felt about her, and now she knew why. Moreover, she recognized the logic and truth in his words. The argument that she did contribute by cleaning, cooking, and generally taking care of the house wasn't completely valid, because she did it for Lije. If it weren't for her husband, she would never have ventured into this country. She had always believed that she was a city person. And Jim Two Pony had recognized that instinctively.

At the evening meal, Diana picked at the food she had so carefully prepared. She tried to follow the conversation between Lije and Jim, but there were too many terms that she didn't understand. Her fear of the widening gap with Lije stole her appetite. She kept wondering how long it would be before Lije noticed the differences between them.

Usually Diana waited until the men finished their coffee before clearing the table, but tonight she couldn't sit passively in her chair and wait. Gray eyes watched her thoughtfully as she made the trips back and forth between the sink and the table. Even after Jim left the kichen to check on one of their mares who was sick, Lije stayed at the table, not retreating to his desk in the living room as he usually did.

"Is anything the matter, Diana?" he asked quietly when the silence continued.

She became conscious of a tear slowly wandering down her cheek. She wiped it away with a soapy hand as she vigorously shook her head that nothing was wrong. There was the scraping of his chair on the floor and footsteps bringing Lije to the sink.

"Then what's that teardrop doing on your cheek?" A finger touched her other cheek. Diana moved her face against his hand, seeking the comfort of his caress. She turned her jewel-bright eyes to look at him.

"Why are you crying?" Lije asked gently.

She swallowed the lump in her throat, then smiled. "Because I'm not a yucca plant, I guess."

"What are you talking about, darling?" He smiled back at her, but there was a puzzled light in his eyes.

"Oh...." Diana hesitated. She didn't know whether or not she should tell him of her discussion with Jim. For some reason she was afraid. "It was just some silliness." She laughed shakily.

"Are you sure?"

"Yes, I'm sure," she nodded.

"Why don't you let those dishes be for a while?" His arms circled her waist as he nuzzled her ear. "We'll build a fire in the fireplace."

"Don't you have paperwork to do?"

She was held tightly against him, but she continued to stare at the sink full of dishes. She was becoming overconscious of taking Lije away from his work.

"Not tonight." he whispered in her ear.

With those beautiful words she turned in his arms to face him, her love shining brilliantly out of her eyes. She needed him so much.

"Hold me, Lije," she murmured fervently.

Her happiness seemed like a very elusive thing.

CHAPTER EIGHT

A FEW DAYS LATER Cord Harris telephoned and made arrangements to fly up in his private plane the following weekend. Lije and Jim both spent extra time with the yearlings he wanted to show Cord. When Cord had learned of their recent marriage, he stated that he would bring his wife with him. Not until Diana learned that Stacy was coming did she realize how much she had missed contact with other women.

When the morning came for the Harrises' arrival, Diana's enthusiasm had her hearing the drone of an airplane motor half a dozen times before the red Cessna aircraft actually flew over the ranch. She raced out of the house to intercept Lije, who was just crawling into the jeep to go out to meet them.

"Can I come with you?" she asked breathlessly. Her face was aglow with excitement.

"Hop in." The gray eyes smiled as Diana quickly took the seat beside him.

They rattled over the track leading to the flat stretch of pasture where a lonely red wind sock marked the landing area. Diana could barely conceal her impatience as the plane slowly taxied to where she and Lije were parked. She quickly followed Lije when he hopped out from behind the wheel and walked to meet the man and woman stepping out of the plane.

Stacy's twinkling brown eyes sought Diana out immediately. As she gave her a quick hug, Stacy whispered, "I feel like a matchmaker. Congratulations, although I think I'm supposed to say that to the bridegroom."

"Thank you." The warm feeling of friendliness brought a sparkle of happy tears to Diana's eyes. "I'm glad you could come."

"Cord is very thoughtful that way." Stacy glanced at her husband talking to Lije before smiling back at Diana. "He knew this trip would break the monotony of ranch life for you as well as me, although I'm already getting homesick for little Josh."

All the way back to the ranch yard, the two women chattered about the little boy while the men sat in front wrapped up in ranch talk. When Lije stopped the jeep near the corrals, Cord turned around to look at Stacy.

"I want you to see the stallion Lije has, Stacy. Malpais is a fabulous animal," said Cord.

"I'll have Jim bring him out of his paddock so you can have a closer look, Stacy," Lije offered, signaling to Jim Two Pony just walking out to greet them.

The big, barrel-chested bay was led out for their inspection. Diana listened with envy as Stacy led the discussion in admiring the muscular haunches that could spring the horse into full speed in one bounding leap, and the beautifully formed head with its dignified, intelligent brown eyes. Diana wished she was as well versed in the finer points of the quarter horse as Stacy was. But then it was quite obvious that Stacy was a horsewoman, while she, Diana thought with a wry smile, was a "housewoman."

The stallion was led back to its enclosure and the yearlings were paraded for Cord one at a time. Diana watched the proceedings, not understanding why three were singled out over what seemed to her equally beautiful horses. When Cord and Lije became engaged in a purely business discussion, Stacy suggested that she and Diana walk over the corral to look at the older horses.

"That's a beautiful chocolate-colored mare!" Stacy exclaimed excitedly.

"Which one?" Diana asked. She couldn't tell a mare from a stallion and all the horses looked brown to her.

"That one there." Stacy pointed, "with the star on her forehead and the white front foot. She's a dainty little horse. Cord, come and look at this mare!"

The two men walked over to where the women stood near the corral. Diana had finally been able to determine which horse Stacy was talking about and admitted silently that it was a pretty horse, with soft, intelligent brown eyes. Lije opened the corral gate and walked over to the mare, taking her by the halter and leading her to the railing where Stacy waited.

"How old is she?" Cord's keen eyes trailed over the horse.

"A coming four-year-old," Lije answered. "Would you like to ride her, Stacy?"

"Would I ever!" Stacy laughed as Lije turned to ask Jim to saddle the horse. The brunette turned her laughing gaze to include Diana and Cord. "I have a horse of my own, but Cord won't let me ride him. I've been trying to find another horse that's spirited enough for me and gentle enough for him to approve."

"She looks like an ideal ladies' mount," Cord agreed, watching the mare standing quietly as Jim tightened the saddle cinch. "I wouldn't get too enthusiastic about her, Stacy; Lije might want to keep her for Diana."

"Oh, no." Diana spoke up quickly as Lije turned a questioning look on her. "I don't ride."

"You'll have to get Lije to teach you," Stacy said, putting her foot in the stirrup while Jim held the horse's head. "There's nothing like exploring this kind of rugged country from the back of a horse."

Diana smiled, but didn't reply as she watched Stacy expertly put the mare through her paces with the wild landscape as a backdrop. The thought of riding alone out in that country intimidated her, and especially on the back of a horse. Her mind conjured up all kinds of images—rattlesnakes, coyotes, mountain lions, jagged cliffs.

"She's perfect!" Stacy exclaimed, dismounting and hugging the mare briefly before dancing over to her husband. "You do like her, don't you?"

The way he looked back at Stacy gave Diana the impression that if she and Lije weren't there, he would have taken his wife in his arms. As it was, Cord just smiled and nodded. "As if I could refuse you!"

"Diana and I will go up to the house while you persuade Lije to sell her." And Diana was swept away with the exuberant Stacy toward the house.

"I wish I were more like you," Diana sighed after she had put the coffee pot on and joined Stacy at the kitchen table.

"What do you mean?"

"You're so at home on the ranch. You know one end of a horse from the other and you ride. About the only thing countrified about me is my denim jeans." Diana tried to laugh at herself. "How did you make the adjustment from big city life?"

"I traveled a great deal with my father, and not always to populated areas, so I was partially accustomed to remote areas," Stacy explained. "And my father had a love affair with nature, which he passed on to me."

"Is the part of Texas where your ranch is very different from here?"

"It isn't quite as untamed as this." The glowing expression on Stacy's face revealed her admiration for the one quality about Diana's new home that Diana herself most disliked. "It really takes a rugged individualist to carve out a place for himself in this kind of wilderness.''

"Don't you get worried sometimes when Cord goes out on the range?''

"Yes, sometimes,'' Stacy grinned. ''It's foolish I know, but I think it's natural that you would worry about the one you love.''

"Lije goes out by himself a lot.'' Diana stared out the window, remembering the long, lonely hours she spent watching for him to return safely. "We're so far away from any kind of help. It worries me just thinking how critical that could be if there were ever an emergency.''

"Don't borrow trouble, Diana.'' Stacy touched the hands clutched so tensely on the tabletop.

"The coffee is done.'' Diana hopped nervously up from the table. Yet it seemed so natural to confide in Stacy, especially since she understood so well. "I made a coffee cake. Would you like a slice?''

"No, thanks.'' Stacy refused with a laugh. "I still have a few pounds I'm trying to shed after the baby.''

"Your figure looks marvelous to me.''

"There are still a few of my clothes that are a little tight. A reminder that my girlish figure isn't quite back to its former slimness.''

"I've put on a couple of pounds, too.'' Diana glanced down at her plaid slacks, a finger sliding into the waistband that hugged her tightly. "I've been overdoing the baking lately and sampling too much of the results, I guess.''

"On you it looks good," the other girl commented. "Being a model you probably had to stay as skinny as you could for the camera's sake."

"It was getting harder and harder to do, too," Diana replied wryly. "I kept developing curves."

"Have you got a couple of cups of that coffee for us?" Lije demanded in a teasing voice as he and Cord walked in the door.

"Of course." Diana was quick to place two more cups on the table along with the plates for the coffee cake, which she sat in the center.

"The mare is yours now," Cord said quietly as he sat beside his wife. Her mouth formed the words "thank you" from amid a glowing smile.

"I have to pick up the Hereford bull I bought, so I've agreed to trailer the horses Cord bought to his ranch. Then I can bring the bull back in the empty trailer." Lije's statement was addressed to both women, but Diana knew it was specifically meant for her.

Although he had never mentioned the possibility of Cord's buying any of his yearlings since that day in San Antonio, Diana had known instinctively that Lije had counted on it. Without the money from that sale, he had been reluctant to buy the bull he needed for his herd. It would have been too much of a strain on their financial resources. So while she silently rejoiced with him, she also looked forward to his coming journey with trepidation. It would be their first separation, which in itself would be a pull on her heartstrings, but it was being left alone on the ranch that she dreaded more.

It was some time later when Cord rose from the table, signaling his wife that it was time for them to be on their way. Diana insisted on refilling their thermos of coffee and preparing sandwiches for their plane ride home, stating that it was the least she could do since they weren't able to stay for a meal. Neither Cord nor Stacy put up any argument. Stacy stayed with Diana to lend assistance while her husband and Lije went out to "pre-flight" the plane.

"Do you think you can persuade Lije to let you come with him when he brings the horses?" Stacy sliced efficiently at the cold roast beef while Diana cut generous portions of her homemade bread.

"If I asked him, he would. But as much as I would like to, I won't." Her blue eyes turned apologetically toward Stacy. "Without me along he'll probably drive right through, settling for a nap in the cab of the truck. If I were with him, he would feel obliged to stop at a motel. And I would know, no matter how well he would hide it, that he was anxious to get back to the ranch." Diana sighed. "I'll stay home like a good rancher's wife."

"Diana." Stacy laid the knife down and turned to the bent blond head that revealed, just as the wry bitterness in her last words had done, Diana's resigned acceptance of her decision. "I know this life and this country must seem strange to you. It's only because it's different from what you've known. It's perfectly natural for people to be apprehensive and even dislike things they don't know about. This ranch and the land must seem like a godforsaken place to you.''

Stacy's words were so accurate that an ironic smile tilted the corners of Diana's mouth. ''Godforsaken'' was such an appropriate word.

''It isn't.'' Stacy's voice was lowered in her earnestness to get her new friend to understand. ''This is probably one of the more God-beloved parts of our country. Nothing is what it seems on the surface. You must get closer and inspect it, see how it lives and grows. Unseeing eyes look at this land and perceive a wild, rugged and harsh place that's forbidding and hauntingly beautiful at the same time. You must open your eyes and see not just the grotesque caterpillar, but the butterfly, as well.''

''I know what you're saying is probably true, but how can I do it? I'm not like you. I don't ride, and once out of sight of the house, I'm lost. The only vehicles we have are the jeep and the pickup. I doubt whether I could drive either one,'' she answered.

''Have you ever been outside the ranch yard?''

''No.''

''Then ask your husband to take you around, to show you the ranch.'' Stacy held Diana's hands, which were still trying to slice more bread. ''This is your home now. It would be a natural request.''

''Lije is so busy. He has so much to do that I don't want to interfere with his work.'' Diana shook her head.

''You wouldn't be. Don't you see? There would

be things he could do, too. Check on fences, and waterholes, predators. A hundred things, I'm sure, and at the same time he would be showing you the country. Promise me you'll do it, Diana," Stacy implored. "And look beneath the strangeness of the land."

"I promise," she agreed, unable to do anything else in the face of those caring brown eyes and the friendly sprinkling of freckles. Immediately there spread across Stacy's face a grin that was filled with impish fun.

"I do hope you were cutting some of this bread for yourself, because Cord and I can't possibly eat that much," she said.

Diana looked with surprise at the towering slices of bread before joining in with the other girl's laughter. The light touch relaxed the tension that had been building up inside her. She was still smiling when Cord and Lije returned from the plane, but with their entrance, depression settled once again. Stacy was leaving and there was no way of knowing when she would see her again.

The ride from the ranch yard to where the plane was parked seemed extremely short. The smile on Diana's lips was forced, as was the gay wave of her hand in a last goodbye to the couple in the plane. A lump rose in her throat as the plane turned and made its run down the grass strip. When the wheels left the ground, she felt her last contact with civilization had just been broken and she was left behind in this desolate land.

As the red object winged out of sight, Diana

turned to the man standing beside her. Blue eyes
looked at the harsh, uncompromising lines of his
face. It was during moments like these when the
alienness of her surroundings overwhelmed her
that her husband seemed a total stranger to her
and not the man she snuggled against at night.

"The excitement is over. It's back to just us
now," Lije said quietly.

"Yes," Diana sighed heavily. Lije moved toward the jeep. "I think . . . I think I'll walk back to
the house."

"Don't be ridiculous! It's too far to walk. Get in
the jeep." The reprimand and order were snapped
out with the autocratic ease of one accustomed to
being obeyed.

Lije was already sitting stiffly behind the wheel
when Diana made slow, reluctant movements to
join him. There was an awkward stony silence between them. Diana didn't want to give voice to her
thoughts. She had been so sure of her ability to
adapt to her new home and its surroundings, and
in Stacy's presence she had been more than hopeful that her new friend's advice would work. Now,
looking at the emptiness of the horizon, she
doubted that anything could bring her to like this
barren land when she couldn't even do it with the
strength of her love for her husband.

"I can't make it any easier for you, Diana."

The jeep was halted in the yard. His words fore-
stalled her movements to leave the vehicle as her
head jerked around to face him.

"What are you talking about?" The murmured

question was directed at the cold glitter in his eyes.

"I can't count the number of times I've seen that mask steal over your face to prevent me from seeing what you think and feel." Diana winced inwardly at his cutting tone. "I thought this visit would help, but it's only made it worse, hasn't it?"

"Lije?" The apology was forming, but he didn't give her an opportunity to complete it.

"Why don't you just admit that you're homesick for the excitement of city life and stop trying to kid both of us?" he snapped.

"All right, I am," she retorted sharply, stung by his sudden attack. "But that doesn't change anything. I'll get over it."

"Will you?" An eyebrow was raised mockingly over his disbelieving gaze. "Some women never adjust to country life. They end up resenting their husbands for forcing them to lead such an isolated existence and hating them when they won't leave it. Divorce is inevitable in those cases."

"Is that what you think is going to happen with us?" Diana gasped in shocked but suppressed anger. The carved profile was turned toward the distant mountains and she couldn't see the expression on his face.

"Why couldn't you talk to me about the way you feel?" Lije's voice was cold as a mountain stream. "Why did you discuss it with a virtual stranger instead of me?"

"You mean Stacy?" The flint gray eyes turned accusingly on her at the question. "She's a woman. She would understand how I felt, having more or less made the transition herself," Diana explained defensively. "I didn't want to worry you or add to your burden. How did you know I'd talked to her?"

"I'm not so selfish and blind that I don't know what a difficult adjustment you've had to make," Lije sneered. "And I've been around enough married couples to know the compassion that springs into a woman's eyes when the wife confides what a rotten life she has."

"Rotten life?" Diana exclaimed angrily. "I love you, Lije Masters!"

"Love can happen between two people at the wrong place and time." That terrible remoteness was in his face as if the distance between them was a hundred times more than the few inches that separated them in the jeep. And his voice was ominously soft. "I told you even before the subject of marriage was brought up how much this ranch meant to me. I love you, Diana, but I would *never* give it up even for you."

"I know that." Did she, she asked herself. Or had she subconsciously hoped that some day she might be able to persuade him differently? She was so upset and confused she couldn't think straight. She hated arguing, and this argument was making her feel physically ill. She seized on the subject of the ranch in a last attempt at placating his cold anger, however justified. "I...I've never seen the ranch. I...I mean, you've never taken me around and shown it to me. Would you?"

"I'll be too busy the next couple of weeks with

the horses and so on, but Jim will be checking the fences. He can take you with him if you really want to go." Lije's hand was massaging the back of his neck as he growled his reply.

"No." Diana refused too quickly, bringing the sharp, condemning look back in his eyes. "I'd rather go with you when you have time."

"I thought you'd got over the ridiculous prejudice toward Jim," he observed contemptuously.

"I'm not prejudiced," Diana protested. "It's just that Jim doesn't like me."

"I think it's you who don't like Jim rather than the reverse."

"Lije, I don't know him well enough to like or dislike him." Diana's shoulders lifted in an uncertain shrug. "Knowing how he feels toward me makes me uncomfortable to be with him. Besides, this ranch is where we live and I want *you* to show it to me, not some man who works for you."

"You make him sound like a servant instead of my friend." His eyes had narrowed to glittering slits of silver gray.

"You're misunderstanding everything I say."

"Am I?" he jeered.

"Why are you acting this way?" She swallowed desperately at the growing lump in her throat and the sobbing pain centered around her heart. "What great sin have I committed, to make you so cold and remote?"

Her questions might never have been asked for all the attention Lije gave them.

"Why did you tell Stacy what you should have discussed with me first?" he demanded.

"Is that what's bothering you? Just that I happened to question Stacy about what had helped her to adjust to ranch life?"

"I suppose it was Stacy who prompted your sudden interest in seeing the ranch after more than a month has gone by since we arrived."

His sarcastic comment brought a scarlet color to her cheeks. Put that way, it sounded like an unforgivable omission on her part. And in part it was, although Diana was too hurt to concede that.

"I don't understand you," she murmured.

"How could you?" There was an arrogant coolness in his voice and face. "After all, out of the three days before we were married, we were only in each other's company about twelve hours in all. Hardly sufficient time to discover whether I'm the person you want to spend the rest of your life with, is it?"

"Are you trying to suggest that I made a mistake?" she breathed.

A weary expression clouded the already gray eyes that Lije turned toward her. "It's possible we both made a mistake. But if it's anybody's fault, it's mine. I knew the kind of life I was bringing you to. But then it's gone beyond the point where it's easily corrected, hasn't it?"

Diana made an instinctive movement toward him, aching to assure him of the depth of her love. Words eluded her, since so much of what he was saying was beyond her understanding. Yet something in his expression prevented her from touching him.

"Neither one of us is capable of carrying on a rational conversation right now," Lije inserted before Diana had a chance to argue. "We're too emotionally involved."

He turned the key in the ignition switch and started the motor of the jeep. Diana felt as if he had patted her head and told her to run along like a good little girl. She did relinquish her passenger seat and dash toward the house, but with bitter tears stinging her eyes.

Over the next few days an air of normalcy existed, at least on the surface. But there was an underlying current of tension that tugged at the precariously floating foundation of Diana's happiness. Lije didn't bring up the subject of their marriage again, but their unspoken thoughts crackled in the air between them. While Diana was relieved that there wasn't an open rift between them, she was also more guarded in displaying her feelings. Yet that very act frightened her, because it seemed to prove that they had a severe communication gap. It was one she didn't want to bridge for fear of the consequences.

By the conversation between Lije and Jim Two Pony at the dinner table, Diana knew it was lambing season. Her husband's days were spent away from the ranch yard and the twilight hours were devoted to the horses, with the paperwork claiming the remaining evening. So there was little real opportunity for serious discussions. Diana was usually in bed, feigning sleep, when Lije would at last enter the bedroom.

Even after the weight of his body had sunk into the mattress beside her, she did not fall asleep, but lay awake listening to his rhythmical breathing. When sleep did claim her, it was troubled by nightmares where Lije was in peril and only she could save him. But always her limbs were frozen into immobility by her terror. In the morning she would awake with the sickening nausea of her failure still clinging to her.

During the long daylight hours when she was left alone with her thoughts, Diana felt as if they were two strangers living under the same roof, barely seeing or speaking to each other except in passing. She hadn't even had the courage to ask again about seeing the rest of the ranch, coming to the conclusion that Stacy's suggestion would only lead to more arguments. And she hadn't recovered from the wounds of the last.

CHAPTER NINE

THE MORNING SKY was an immense stretch of startling blue that seemed to belong to an artist's canvas. The sun was a glaring yellow orb suspended over the distant mountains, casting long black shadows over the uneven terrain. A hawk soared lazily overhead, its wide wingspan catching the unseen wind currents. The coolness of the mountain night lingered, turning the warm breath of the horses in the corral to smoky puffs.

Her hands were shoved deep in the pockets of her tan jacket as Diana stared at the strange landscape. There was resentment in her aquamarine eyes that such a vast amount of space could constitute her prison walls. She had not even the means to escape because Lije had the pickup truck and Jim had the jeep.

Exhaustion caused by nights of restless sleep painted pale blue circles under her eyes, giving them a haunted look. At the same time, Diana couldn't relax during the day, constantly being driven by the nervous energy that kept her physically active.

She stared at the weathered house and outbuildings in sullen silence. A debate went on inside her whether or not to take the paint out of the store-room and paint them herself just for something to do before she shrugged the thought away in a moment of pique. That was her husband's responsibility.

Letting her wandering pace carry her to the rear of the house, Diana watched the movement of her shiny brown shoes, the toes already showing a covering of pale dust. A cynical smile curled the corners of her mouth as she realized what an incongruous picture she made in this backdrop of rugged country.

Crinkling and shiny brown patent leather shoes on her feet were very practical for walking long blocks on city sidewalks, but they were useless in this terrain where rocks and thorny bushes would scratch and mar their shiny surface. The beautifully tailored brown slacks molded her slender long legs and enhanced the provocative curve of her hips, but the material would snag at the slightest touch. Certainly not the attire to tramp this countryside. The tan jacket covering her white silk overblouse was designed for looks and not warmth, which, with the promise of springtime weather, was not too bad. Still, Diana thought, she looked like exactly what she was—a model placed in a Western setting instead of the usual cardboard backdrop.

What was that Stacy had said? East is east and west is west and never the twain shall meet. Diana was beginning to believe that was the rule and Stacy had been the exception to prove it. It was hardly an encouraging thought.

Her restless feet had carried her to the small rise behind the house. A distant spiky-leafed plant with a towering center stalk beckoned her, an instant reminder of Jim Two Pony's comparison of a yucca plant and a rose. His description of the yucca fitted the plant she was looking at and she walked toward it for a closer inspection. There were no bell-shaped flowers on the stalk, only a dense gathering of barely formed buds.

Further on there were more such plants firmly rooted in a rocky hillside. Diana walked toward them, pausing once to look back at the house to make sure it was in sight. The dark roof was plainly visible. A long-legged rabbit hopped briskly away as Diana approached a heavy growth of vegetation. His hasty departure gave rise again to her own desire to flee her unfriendly surroundings. With a resigned sigh, she continued on. The top of a larger hill promised a more encompassing view of the land that she was trying to reconcile herself to accept as home.

When Diana attained her new vantage point, she gazed out over the awesome stretch of uncivilized land. Far, far away, she could see dark specs of slowly moving animals. She remembered vaguely Lije mentioning that the cattle were still pastured near the house and assumed that what she saw was part of the herd. The minute appearance the distance gave them made her more fully aware of her own insignificance, and a chill brought on by the loneliness of her existence sent a shiver through her body. She looked back at the square building that was her home, so very different from the images she had dreamed.

Subconsciously Diana knew she had wandered as far from the house as she dared, that now was the time to turn back, but she could not face returning to that drab interior that always seemed to contribute to her depression. Instead she made her way down the opposite side of the hill, convincing herself that as long as she kept the hill in sight, she wouldn't get lost.

By nature Diana had never been adventurous, only curious, but her situation seemed desperate. Regardless of the negative side that brushed off Stacy's suggestion of investigating the ranch as not being the solution, Diana was driven to explore all possibilities. This inner compulsion led her down a small draw at the base of the hill, confident that she had only to retrace her steps to be back at her starting point.

None of the plant or animal life that she saw was any that she had seen before. Except for the yucca plants that Jim Two Pony had described to her, she could only guess that the scrubby-looking trees she saw belonged to the pine family. The clumps of underbrush were a complete mystery to her. There wasn't a sign of a robin or blue jay or English sparrow, and definitely not the pigeons that abounded in the tall concrete cities she knew.

The landscape was painted in earth tones from the dark dull green of the piny needles on umber-colored branches to the cinnamon- and ocher-colored rocks amid the pale sandy soil. Distant mountain peaks were a peculiar purple brown. The vivid blue of the sky and the yellow glint of the sun in her eyes were the only bold colors in the otherwise drab and somber land.

An animal trail led from the base of the draw to its rim some five feet above. Diana made her way warily up its steep incline, her mind imagining the animals that might have used it before her. With visions of coyotes and mountain lions dancing in her head, it was something of a start for Diana to reach the top and find herself staring at a white-faced cow. She took a hasty step backward, nearly losing her balance before she stopped. The cow eyed her suspiciously for several seconds more, then it turned and trotted hastily away. Not until there was no further chance that it might return did Diana expel the breath she had unknowingly been holding.

Still Diana didn't immediately turn back. The muscles in the calves of her legs were aching from the unaccustomed climbing she had been doing. To the right of where the cow had been standing was a jumble of rocks. One flat rock looked inviting, offering a relatively comfortable seat when compared to the grass and brush-covered earth. When Diana climbed onto the flat rock, she discovered that while the rock rising behind it was jagged and rough, she could position herself to avoid the sharper edges and obtain a suitable back rest. The rays of the sun had given the stony surface a pleasant warmth that made it doubly relaxing. Leaning back, Diana closed her eyes and basked in the continued sunlight.

A FLY MADE lazy tracks across her cheek. Her hand moved up and brushed the pesky insect away, but it determinedly buzzed around her face. Blinking hastily, Diana realized she had dozed off. She glanced quickly at her wrist before she realized she had left her watch on the counter by the kitchen sink. The sun didn't seem to have changed its position very much, hanging a little higher in the sky. A vague gnawing in her stomach confirmed that it was close to lunchtime.

The path leading back down the draw was farther away than she had first thought. But the sun that had been over her shoulder during the first part of her walk was now shining in her eyes as she began to retrace her steps. Her legs were a little stiff and she felt the beginnings of a blister on her heel. The nagging discomfort increased as she kept walking down the draw with still not a sign of the hill that would bring her in sight of the house. If it weren't for the sun still reassuringly shining in front of her, she would have begun to believe that she had taken a wrong turning and was lost.

The teasing breeze carried a sound to her. At first Diana had the strange feeling that someone had called her name before she shrugged it off as one of those peculiar bird calls. Several feet farther, the rhythmic and muffled beat of an animal approaching from behind her reached her ears. With the memory of coming unexpectedly on the cow still fresh in her mind, she paused and turned toward the sound. Her hand brushed the feathery strands of silver gold hair away from her eyes as she peered earnestly toward the continuing sound.

The walls of the draw seemed to draw closer, making its confines become very narrow. The idea of becoming the obstacle in the path of an unknown animal became a more pronounced possibility as the sound drew closer. The sides were steep, but Diana didn't really care. She raced to the side, her eyes desperately scanning for a foothold or a handhold that would take her to the top, but her inexperienced eyes saw none. Glancing nervously over her shoulder at the bend in the draw, she saw a horse and rider walk slowly around the bend. Her thudding heart slowed in relief.

"Lije!" she called weakly but gaily.

"What the hell are you doing?" he barked, reining his horse to a stop beside her and glowering down at her upturned face.

With that cold remote expression in his eyes, Diana couldn't bring herself to tell him that she had been about to claw her way out of the draw. He was not in a mood to laugh anything off.

"I was going for a walk." In spite of her resolve to keep things light, a defensive note crept into her voice.

"Did you have any particular destination in mind?" Lije asked grimly.

"As a matter of fact, I was just on my way back to the house."

"The house is that way." He pointed in the direction he had just come.

"That's impossible." A troubled, disbelieving expression creased her forehead. "The sun was behind me when I started and now it's in front of me."

"What time is it?"

"I. . .I left my watch by the sink."

"It happens to be two o'clock in the afternoon, and the sun does move to the west in the afternoon."

Her mouth opened and closed as she tried to think of some reply that wouldn't make her sound as ignorant as she was.

"Do you have any idea how close you came to really getting lost?" Lije demanded. Mutely Diana nodded as the realization began to sink in. "If I hadn't come back to the house at noon and couldn't find you. . . ." He left the thought hanging in the air. "Damn it, Diana! What if I hadn't come back until nightfall? Didn't you even notice that you weren't going back the same way?"

"Everything out here looks strange to me." She lowered her head to prevent Lije from seeing her trembling chin.

The creak of saddle leather announced that Lije was dismounting. Diana didn't feel any safer as he towered beside her. The pain her chest was becoming so intense that she had to laugh or she would cry. What started out as a throaty chuckle quickly turned into hysterical laughter, and not even Lije's fingers digging into her shoulders as he shook her penetrated her consciousness. It took a stinging slap across her face before the hysteria abated.

"Don't you see how funny it is?" she demanded, a wild glitter still in her eyes. "I didn't know east from west even when the sun was shining!"

"Get a hold of yourself!"

His hand gripped the back of her neck, forcing her face up toward his. The forbidding expression on his face was far from soothing. For the first time, Diana found herself struggling to free herself from her husband's arms.

"Let me go!" she hissed. Lije was caught off guard, relaxing his hold just long enough for Diana to slip away. Her action was unnatural, but the long-held-in emotions and pent-up frustrations had her standing in trembling anger before him. "Don't touch me," she murmured furiously as his hand moved again toward her shoulder.

If Diana had considered Lije's previous expression as forbidding, now he looked decidedly intimidating. And her hastily spoken words had goaded his already growing anger into full fire.

"I haven't touched you for nearly a week," he snarled, his hands bringing her rigid body against the solidness of his. Her face was turned mutinously toward him, refusing to submit to this threatening pose.

"It's amazing you could suppress—" Diana began sarcastically, only to be interrupted by a muttered expletive from Lije before his mouth brutally covered hers.

The savagery of his embrace didn't hold the slightest hint of passion or desire. Diana was locked against the granite-hard muscles of his chest by two iron bands that constricted until there was no air left in her lungs. The unrelenting kiss pressed her lips against her teeth with such force that it split the underside of her lip, leaving the salty taste of blood in her mouth. The throbbing in her temples increased and blackness swarmed in front of her eyes as she felt herself ready to faint from the lack of oxygen. With her arms pinned to her sides, her struggles were pitifully weak.

Then she was standing free, gulping in the sweet breath of life. Feeling returned to her numbed arms and legs and her lips still felt the vicious bruising of his kiss. The pain was just beginning to recede in her forehead as she slowly opened her eyes and let her icy blue gaze meet the remarkable blandness of his.

"You brute!" she whispered vehemently, startled to see his mouth twitch with mocking amusement. "And wipe that smile off your face!"

"Surely your twisted sense of humor sees the funny side of this," Lije jeered. "I nearly raped my wife."

Her face paled as a hundred angry, spiteful words rose to her throat, each fighting with the other so that none of them came out. Pivoting sharply, Diana stalked away from him, uncaring of the direction or the terrain.

"Unless you're running away, the house is still in the opposite direction."

His softly spoken yet mocking voice brought her up short. But her pride refused to let her turn around. It was foolish to continue on and get herself genuinely lost.

"Diana, we both rather exploded today when the strain of these last few days became too much. Let's leave it at that." His quiet voice carried the autocratic ring of command. "I want you to walk back to the house with me."

She knew it was the closest to an apology she was going to get in the circumstances. She had to admit that a lot of her anger had been caused by the tension and frustration. But all the logical thinking one part of her brain did was offset by the still smoldering resentment nurtured by the other half. Diana turned around and walked back to Lije, refusing to meet his eyes or look at him even when he turned away from her to take the reins of his horse, leading it as they started back.

The silence between them was magnified by the shuffling sound of the horse's hooves on the sandy ground. The firm tilt of her chin and the squared shoulders were reminiscent of earlier childhood scenes when she had been hurt by those she had wanted to please. A capricious wind danced with the long silken strands of her hair, uncaring that gray eyes watched its intimate play.

"The next time you go for a walk," Lije broke the silence, "I suggest you pick out landmarks, whether it's a mountain peak, a peculiar rock formation, or a twisted pine tree. When you've walked past them, turn around and see what they look like from the other direction. Landscapes appear totally different when viewed from the opposite direction. Leave a note to say which direction you're going. Just don't go wandering off like that again, Diana.''

She nodded brisky. It wasn't necessary to add that, at the moment, more explorations were the last thing on her mind.

"All the arrangements have been completed. I have to pick up the health certificates on the horses this afternoon, which means I'll be leaving the day after tomorrow to deliver the horses to Cord," Lije went on. "Will you be all right while I'm gone?"

His solicitous questions amused her as brittle laughter rolled briefly from her throat. She let her gaze move up to his.

"I've managed to get by by myself for quite a few years." Her voice sounded colder and more independent than Diana meant it to be, but she didn't regret it, not even when he regarded her through narrowed eyes.

"When I get back, I'll take you on that tour of the ranch." The statement was drawn out of the grim line made by his mouth.

Diana was prevented from flinging the offer back in his face by a third voice coming from the hilltop where her walk had started.

"You found her already," Jim Two Pony said.

"She hadn't gone very far," Lije replied, while Diana surveyed the two in tight-lipped silence. "She was walking along the wash."

"It isn't good for her to wander out of sight of the house." The Navaho fell into step beside Lije as they topped the rise and started down toward the dark roof of the house.

"I think she learned her lesson."

"Will you two stop talking about me as if I were some dumb animal incapable of speech!" Diana demanded shrilly. "Or do you both consider me as a prize mare to be cosseted and admired, but never to be more than a show specimen?"

Not waiting for a reply, she quickened her stride, letting it carry her ahead of them. Any moment she expected Lije to catch up with her and let his displeasure at her rudeness be known, but he didn't.

A DREARY GRAY DAWN muted the morning calls of the early-rising birds as Lije rechecked the lashings of the horses in the van before locking the door. The remnants of the briskly cool night air made his movements crisp and hurried to keep the coldness from nibbling at an unmoving limb. Diana watched his progress from the kitchen window, her quilted robe clutched together with one hand. When he turned toward the house, she quickly busied herself with the coffee pot, pouring herself a cup and retreating to the table. A rush of cold air raced in as Lije walked in the door.

"Do you want another cup of coffee before you leave?" Diana asked quietly, observing the unspoken rules of their truce.

He stood just inside the door, his cynical gaze taking in her perfectly poised features. "No." He reached for the thermos sitting on the counter near the door. "It's time for me to leave."

Yet he made no move toward the door, his eyes holding hers in a compelling gaze. Diana knew what he was thinking—that she didn't have the nerve to carry out the mockery of their goodbye to its final stage. Striving for all the nonchalance she could obtain, she rose from her chair and walked to him, fighting the desire to slap the ridiculing expression off his face, as well as wishing he would take her in his arms and kiss her the way he used to do.

"Drive carefully, Lije," she instructed, rising on tiptoe to brush her lips against his.

Before she could step away, his hand came out to rest on the side of her neck, tilting her chin toward him. The kiss he gave her was firm and possessive, as if to remind her that she belonged to him.

"I'll be back in about four days. Try to miss me while I'm gone."

There was another rush of cold air and Lije was out the door and striding briskly toward the pickup truck with its horse van hitched behind. There wasn't a backward glance or a final wave as Diana watched him leave. It was difficult to ignore the aching void he left in her heart, regardless of any petty quarrel they had had. Both of them just had too much pride.

Surprisingly the morning hours passed rather swiftly, mostly because Diana tried to convince herself that Lije was only out on the range and not journeying away from her. After a lunch of green salad with cheese and crackers, she spread out a jigsaw puzzle that she had found several weeks ago in one of the trunks in the attic. It was a gigantic picture of a European cathedral, which made all the tiny pieces a myriad shades of tan and gold.

In only a matter of moments Diana was completely engrossed in the puzzle's complexities, so completely that she didn't hear the arrival of an automobile in the ranch yard. The loud rap on the door startled her right out of the chair and she walked hesitantly to the door. In all of the time she had lived on the ranch they had not had one single visitor other than Cord and Stacy. The rare people who stopped by for business reasons usually found Lije out in the ranch buildings, discussed whatever it was that had brought them, and left.

So it was with a mixture of excitement and curiosity that Diana opened the door. A man of medium height and build, dressed in a sports suit of plaid slacks and a dark green jacket, stood with his back to the door surveying the ranch buildings. A cream Stetson was pushed back on his head.

"Can I help you?" Diana asked, bringing the man around with a start. He had a wide friendly face with dancing brown eyes. He was in his late twenties.

"I heard Masters had married, but no one told me his wife was so very lovely," the man drawled softly as he let his gaze roam over her in respectful admiration. His hand reached up and deftly removed his hat while he extended his right hand to her. "My name is Ty Spalding. I own about the only well-drilling rig around these parts."

"I'm pleased to meet you, Mr. Spalding," she acknowledged.

"I stopped out to let Lije know that my rig will be free all this week."

"I'm sorry, he isn't here."

"Maybe I could check with him this evening. I know he wanted a new well drilled in the turtleback out in the south section."

"Actually Lije is out of town. He won't be back for a couple of days," Diana explained. "I'm sure my husband probably discussed this with our foreman."

"You mean the Indian?"

Diana was surprised to find herself flinching at the man's condescending tone. "Yes, Jim Two Pony. He's in charge while Lije is gone."

"Well, where could I find him?" A resigned expression turned the corners of his mouth in a grim line as the man named Ty Spalding looked over the ranch yard.

"I'm afraid he's out on the range somewhere checking fences. I'm not certain whether he'll be back before supper or not."

"Here's my card with my home and business telephone number," he said as he reached into his pocket and withdrew a square white card and handed it to her. "Have him give me a call when he gets back."

"I'll do that, Mr. Spalding," Diana smiled, glancing down at the card briefly.

"The name is Ty, ma'am." The cream hat was set back on his head at a rakish angle. "It's been a pleasure meeting you. I hope I get to see more of you in the future."

Diana realized the man was flirting with her in a very subtle way. Yet his obvious discreetness was oddly pleasing, so that instead of being offended, she felt complimented. Her ego had been a bit deflated, but this stranger had just given it the boost it needed. She stood in the door until Ty Spalding had crawled behind the wheel of his car and driven off.

CHAPTER TEN

It was after seven o'clock before Diana saw the jeep parked near the barn, signaling the return of Jim Two Pony. The dinner had been warming on the stove for the last half hour. From the kitchen window she saw that Jim was preparing to feed the horses, which meant at least another three-quarters of an hour before he was done. With a sigh of irritation she walked to the closet and removed her tan jacket.

Her temper was simmering close to the surface when she walked into the barn, where Jim was calmly measuring grain into a collection of buckets. She stopped a couple of feet away, her toe tapping out a nervous tattoo.

"I have dinner ready at the house, Jim," she said, striving to keep her voice calm.

"I thought it would be best if I ate at my place while Lije is gone," he replied, not a break in the rhythm of his work.

"Lije didn't mention that there was going to be any change in the meals." It was difficult talking to someone when he wouldn't even look at you.

"It was my decision."

"It's too bad you didn't consult me, because I

have the food all prepared. And I certainly can't eat all of it by myself," Diana said crossly.

"The horses have to be fed first."

"The food is on the stove." Exasperation rimmed the edges of her words. "In another forty-five minutes it will be dried up."

"The horses have to be fed. They should have been given their grain an hour ago," Jim answered with quiet persistence.

"What has to be done? Maybe I can help?" Diana didn't know what had prompted this unusual offer from herself, but the sudden gleam in the dark eyes that met hers led her to believe that Jim Two Pony expected her to retract it.

"You can take these portions of grain and put one in the manger bins of each stall," he suggested.

Diana hesitated for only a second before reaching down and picking up two of the buckets. Eager, tossing heads leaned as far over the stalls as the wood partitions permitted. The simple task of emptying the grain from the buckets into the square bins demanded that Diana put her arms in the stalls, brushing against the horses' heads that were pushing and butting to get their meal. She eyed the first horse nervously. It looked gentle enough. Taking a deep breath, she pushed the bucket past the inquiring nose and dumped it into the bin. The horse completely ignored her in favor of the more nutritious grain. Diana was filled with triumphant glee when she returned to gather more buckets of grain, but Jim didn't seem to notice. He had finished measuring the buckets of grain and was busy tossing hay into the larger manger bins.

"A man named Ty Spalding called in this afternoon to see Lije," Diana called to the briskly moving man several feet away. "Something about drilling a water well here on the ranch. He asked if you'd call him tonight."

"Spalding was here?" Jim eyed her sharply before a thoughtful look stole over his face.

"Yes. Didn't Lije mention it to you? About the drilling?"

"Spalding had told him his rig wouldn't be free for another week," he answered, resuming his distribution of the hay.

"He told me it was going to be free all this week." Diana emptied the last bucket of grain and turned with a flourish. "Is there a problem?"

"No. It just would have been more convenient if Lije were here." Jim shrugged, ending the conversation in his own enigmatic manner.

"Are we ready to eat now?" Diana cocked her head at him with just a shade of defiance in the pose.

"There's still the stallion to be fed."

"While you take care of him, I'll go and see what I can save of our meal."

There was the faintest trace of a smile around Jim's mouth as he nodded. "I'll be up when I'm finished."

The conversation between them at the table threatened to be as nonexistent as it had been in the past. Diana had thought those brief moments in the barn where they had worked in harmony would have brought an end to these uneasy silences.

"Do you have any family, Jim?" she asked, looking at him with pointed interest. "Brothers? Sisters?"

"I have no brothers or sisters, only some aunts and uncles and cousins."

"Where do they live? Do you get a chance to visit them very often?"

"They live on a reservation in Arizona. I haven't seen them for several years. Not since my mother died."

Slowly, with more precise questions, Diana was able to draw more information from Jim Two Pony. None of his answers were ever specific, but she did perceive a picture of his early life. It was after his father's death in an auto accident that he and his mother had come to this ranch, where she worked as a housekeeper and cook as well as keeping an eye on her son and Lije. Jim did not reminisce as Lije had done of their escapades as boys, summing it up simply that they had grown up together. Although their conversation brought no new startling discoveries, Diana still felt she had pierced some of his reserve.

When the meal was finished and she had risen to do the dishes, Jim went into the living room to telephone Ty Spalding. With his catlike quietness Diana didn't hear him hang up the phone, or walk into the kitchen and out the door. Only the click of the door latch signaled that he had left—apparently not for good, because a few minutes later Diana heard him pounding away with a hammer just outside the house. Wiping her hands on the dish towel, she walked to the door and looked outside. He was standing on a ladder hanging something on the side of the house. Puzzled, Diana slipped into her jacket and stepped outdoors.

"What are you doing?" In the semidarkness of the coming night she tried to discern what the dull gleam was near his hands.

He didn't answer until he had completed his task and started down the ladder. She could see then the thick rope dangling from a large gray bell mounted on the side of the house.

"The sound of a bell ringing carries a long way out here," he said quietly. "If you should ever need Lije or myself when we're out on the range, you can ring the bell."

For a moment Diana was at a loss for words. It was such a simple gesture of kindness on his part that she didn't know quite how to react. Here was her bond, her means of communication when she was left alone for hours at the ranch house. A large metallic clarion that pealed a sense of security.

"Thank you," she whispered fervently.

A bronze hand touched his hat, then he gathered his tools and the ladder and faded into the darkening twilight. How infinitely safer Diana felt looking up at the faint gleam of burnished gray. She was still smiling serenely when she walked back into the house.

THE MORNING SUN broke with brilliant radiance on the eastern horizon. A bubbling effervescence seemed just below the surface of the day as Diana walked out the kitchen door and glanced up at the comforting bell. It was strange, the suggestion of a promise of a new golden happiness that radiated with the sun's rays.

Rolling clouds of dust acted as ancient smoke signals to announce the arrival of a vehicle approaching the ranch yard. Matching the eagerness of the new day, Diana turned toward the car, recognizing it almost instantly as the tan sedan belonging to Ty Spalding. It was nice to have visitors, especially someone as charming as Ty. In only passing thought did she wonder why he was coming to the ranch yard instead of joining his crew at the drilling site.

"Good morning," she called out gaily as the car slowed to a stop a few feet away. "It's going to be a lovely day, isn't it?"

"It does make you believe spring is just on the other side of that mountain." He had stepped out of the car and pulled his gaze away from her inwardly shining face with difficulty to look at the golden-kissed eastern horizon.

"Jim told me this morning that he was meeting your crew to take them out to the drilling site," Diana said, returning their conversation back to practicalities.

"Yes, he did. I was just heading out there myself, but I thought I'd stop and—" He halted, a pair of dancing brown eyes turning on her with marked directness. "The truth is I stopped because I couldn't really believe you were as beautiful as you appeared yesterday. You have my permission to slap my face if you want to."

The audacity of his words brought a quick gasp of surprise before Diana's sense of humor took over and she burst into laughter. His candor and directness were refreshing after being surrounded by the enigmatic remoteness of her husband, especially in the face of their recent quarrels.

"I think I'll reserve the right for a later time," she ended with a laugh.

"I can't bring myself to call you Mrs. Masters. In the first place, it reminds me that you're married, which I would prefer to forget."

"And in the second place?" She tried hard to be properly prim and serious, only to succumb to his teasing and flirtatious spirit.

"In the second place, I'd like to find out what name goes with that face."

"Diana."

"The name of a goddess, what else?" Ty commented with a mocking widening of his brown eyes. "Well, Diana, you can just put Ty Spalding's name on the list with all your other admirers."

"I'm sorry, Ty, but I can't do that." Her expression bordered on teasing and regret. "Since I got married, I only keep a list of my friends."

"That's a pity. I hate to straddle platonic fences."

"It's either the fence or the gate."

A rueful yet respectful gleam entered his eyes at

her gentle and firmly worded statement. "In that case, you tell those other fence sitters to move over, 'cause I'm climbin' on."

"Welcome aboard, friend," Diana smiled, holding out her hand to him, which he shook with a warm grasp. "Do you know that outside of the townspeople we trade with, you're the first person I've met from the area?"

"Then I count myself lucky, real lucky. Come spring and summer is when the socializing starts around here, and you're bound to be gobbled up in all that whirl of activity."

"I can't visualize there ever being a 'whirl of social activity' around here," she laughed.

"That is an exaggeration," Ty admitted. "But in our rural little way, we do all right."

"In that case, come up to the house and have some coffee and sweet rolls while you tell me all about it."

As they walked to the house, Ty gave her a very embroidered account of some of the more widely attended functions in the area. Her previous assessment at their first meeting that Ty Spalding could be a very charming and amusing companion proved doubly correct. Over coffee, his lighthearted conversation kept a smile on her face, and Diana felt more at ease with herself than since the first day she had set foot on the ranch.

"Pardon the pun, but how did Lije manage to 'master' you, Mrs. Masters?" His engaging smile was easy to return.

"He just swept me off my feet," Diana retorted

mischievously, the glow lighting her eyes with jewellike brilliance at the memory of how he had devastated her from the first moment of their meeting.

"I should say how lucky he was—" a rueful chuckle emphasized Ty's words "—but Lije Masters is a man who makes his own luck. Ever since I can remember he's always been king of the mountain. It was inevitable that he came home with a fair-haired queen." His brown eyes flicked around the kitchen. "I imagine you've already made all the plans to redo your rather dismal castle."

Diana glanced around the room with a stranger's eyes, remembering how vivid her distaste had been the first time she had seen it. Pride wouldn't allow her to say that they couldn't afford anything major in the way of redecorating, so she settled for a noncommittal agreement.

"You women have always amazed me. Give a woman a room, some paint and material and she inevitably turns it into a showplace, regardless of any shoestring budget."

His casual statement stunned her. With new eyes she looked around the kitchen, trying to visualize how fresh paint and new curtains would transform the room. Before her assessment was complete, a discreet knock was heard at the door. When Diana recovered her wits enough to walk to the door, she was surprised to see Jim Two Pony standing outside. He never knocked. The question in his dark eyes puzzled her even more.

"Come in." She stepped aside to enforce her unnecessary invitation.

"I noticed Mr. Spalding's car outside," Jim said, venturing no farther than just inside the door. His gaze moved from Diana to the man leaning back in his chair. "I thought perhaps he wanted to discuss something about the drilling."

"Actually, I was on my way out to the site," Ty informed him in an unhurried and condescending manner, "before Diana invited me in for coffee." There was the slightest bristling in his gaze as he saw Jim glance at the empty cup on the table.

"I have to check on the herd near there. I'll follow you out." Jim's face remained impassive despite the crackling tension that had suddenly risen.

"Why don't you have a cup of coffee, Jim?" Diana suggested, glancing from one to the other, uncertain what had caused this friction.

He declined the offer: "I have a great deal to do with Lije gone." The barest softening in his gaze when it turned on her carried a polite but adamant refusal before it turned blandly back to Ty.

Diana could sense the reluctance and irritation that accompanied Ty's slowness in rising from his chair. He hadn't taken one step in the direction of the door as Jim reached out to hold it open for him.

"I'll be outside directly," Ty told Jim, his hat still in his hand.

Jim nodded, glanced briefly at Diana, then walked out the door, closing only the screen door behind him. The smile now on Ty's face held a hint of anger as he looked at Diana.

"I might have known Lije wouldn't leave you here alone without instructing his faithful little watchdog to look after you," he said with a cynical twist to his smile.

His patronizing tone toward Jim Two Pony left a sour taste in Diana's mouth. This was the second time Ty had made a disparaging remark about him. She hadn't liked it the first time and she found herself being more repulsed this time. But Ty took no notice of the withdrawal in her expression.

"Thanks for the coffee, Diana." He sat the hat firmly back on his head. "I'll be seeing you." A wink emphasized the promise in his voice, then he was through the door, walking briskly ahead of Jim.

In that last span of minutes, the golden aura of happiness that had surrounded her morning vanished. As Diana put the dirty coffee cups in the sink, she tried to fight back at the peculiar unsettled feeling. It hadn't just been Ty's offensive remarks toward Jim, although they had definitely taken the edge off her enjoyment of his company.

She turned, leaning her back against the sink, and let her pensive gaze wander over the kitchen. It had been Ty's offhand comment about a woman's redecorating prowess on a limited budget. For the life of her, Diana couldn't see how fresh paint and new curtains would "transform" this disreputable kitchen. The white enamel on the metal stove and cabinets was chipped, but not even repainting would change their appearance enough to make them more attractive to her eyes. As far as she could see, the answer was a new stove and custom-made wooden cabinets, which they could not afford.

Yet the conversation gnawed at her all the rest of the day. The reason why it bothered her remained out of reach, proving just as disconcerting as the conversation. The evening meal of meat loaf, baked potatoes, and baked beans was in the oven and the coleslaw and strawberry pie were in the refrigerator. The table was all set. The prospect of waiting until Jim arrived demanded more from her patience than Diana possessed.

There was no sign of his jeep outside, and with the memory of the previous night's delay to feed the horses still fresh in her mind, Diana slipped on her jacket and walked down to the stables. Questioning whinnies greeted her entrance as the horses stuck their heads out of the rows of stalls. There was something rather welcoming about the sound. With their graceful heads stretched out toward her, large luminous eyes watching her every move, Diana found them less formidable than before.

A soft, inquiring nicker from a sorrel horse nearest her brought her wandering gaze to it. Its ears were pricked forward in anticipation as it stretched its neck toward her. Hesitantly Diana stepped forward, her hand reaching out for the velvet soft nose to nuzzle. The strip of white that raced across the delicate, gazelle-shaped face accented the shimmering brilliance of its red brown coat. The soft brown eyes blinked at her with incredible gentleness in their expression.

"You look like a Bambi fawn," she commented as she stroked the satiny smooth neck, then added with a quiet laugh, "an overgrown fawn!"

She glanced at the storage bins where the grain was kept and wished she had paid closer attention last night when Jim had been measuring out the grain and supplements for each horse. There was really nothing to feeding the horses, as she had discovered. With Lije away, it would have made one less chore for Jim to do.

Her gaze caught a glimpse of hay stacked near the entrance. There was something she could do that didn't require any measurements before feeding. All she had to do was toss some hay into the mangers. Before the decision was fully formed in her mind, she moved to carry it out. She had one side of the row of stalls completed when the sharp clamor of a bell shattered the contented sounds in the barn. It took a full second for Diana to remember the bell that Jim had hung at the house. She dropped the hay in her hands and raced to the open doorway of the barn.

"Jim, I'm down here!" she called, waving to the dark-haired man standing at the house. She waited in the doorway as he walked to meet her. "Is anything wrong?" she asked as he drew nearer.

"I thought you might have gone for another one of your walks." Jim said quietly with just a suggestion of a smile.

"Not after the last time." She shook her head ruefully. She didn't want to remember that other walk and swiftly changed the subject. "I was just giving the horses some hay. I would have given them grain, too, but I didn't know how much to give."

"I'll show you." Jim was already walking by her into the barn. "The phone was ringing when I walked into the house," he said over his shoulder. "It was Lije calling to let you know he would be driving back in the morning."

"When will he get here?" Diana asked eagerly, her heart dropping a bit at not being able to talk to him herself. In spite of the estrangement that marked their parting, she missed him terribly.

"The day after tomorrow, probably in the morning," Jim answered.

"Did you mention that Ty was here to drill the new well?" Why did she ask that, Diana wondered.

"Yes." Jim glanced at her briefly before opening the grain bins and instructing her in the amount of grain and vitamin and mineral supplements to feed the horses.

Diana was pleased to discover that there really wasn't anything difficult about feeding them once she knew how much. And it was a satisfying experience, as well. This time, secure in the knowledge that their meal wasn't burning up in the oven, she accompanied Jim Two Pony when he fed the big bay stallion, Malpais.

He was a beautiful animal—sleek, muscular,

with graceful lines like a Greek statue come to life. Yet for all his size, the stallion was light on his feet, moving playfully around Jim when he entered the sturdy paddock. The full mane and tail and all four legs were jet black, but the rest of his body was the deepest, darkest shade of brown that was still not yet black.

"Where did he get the name Malpais?" Diana asked when Jim had emptied the grain and hay into the manger and walked over to stand beside her.

"Lije mentioned to you about the lava beds on the north border of the ranch, didn't he?"

Vaguely Diana remembered him making some comment about lava beds when they had first met, but she hadn't thought about it further.

"He did mention it once," she nodded. "I have to admit that I wasn't curious about them until now. But what have they got to do with Malpais?"

"'Malpais' is the Spanish word for badlands," Jim explained. "A most descriptive term for the twisting, black river of rock that stretches for miles. The rock is black—or like the stallion, nearly black."

"I had no idea there were volcanoes here," she murmured.

"These lava flows come from the eruptions of Mount Taylor and El Tintero. Their liquid fire spread southward, killing every living thing in its path and destroying anything else. Occasionally the river of lava would split into two streams and leave an oasis of green trees and grass, puny island remnants of productive land. Eventually the lava hardened, but usually from the outside, leaving the lava flowing within to create caverns and ice caves. In places, the roofs of these caves are paper-thin. One step on top and a man could fall through with never a way out. The human eye cannot detect the difference between the solid rock and the treacherous roofs.''

Diana shuddered expressively at the picture he painted.

"Still, it is only one small patch in the whole of New Mexico." There was quiet amusement in his voice. "Just a few miles from the *malpais* is Acoma, the Sky City. Not far from that is El Morro National Monument. There you can see Inscription Rock, where the early Spanish explorers carved their names. I suppose you could call it an early form of graffiti."

Laughter rolled easily from Diana's lips and with more freedom when Jim Two Pony joined in with her. Her blue eyes registered their pleasure when she met his dark gaze. This new camaraderie was a welcome change and one that she enjoyed very much.

CHAPTER ELEVEN

THE BARRIER had been lowered. The first tentative steps toward friendship and respect had been taken between Diana and Jim Two Pony, though the reserve was still there. The final commitment by either one had not yet been made, but for the first time things looked hopeful to Diana. Her smile was infused with the growing warmth she felt toward the black-haired Navaho as he turned the ignition key in the jeep.

"I'll feed the horses for you tonight if you don't mind," she offered, raising her voice to make sure it would carry over the noise of the motor.

"You can leave Malpais for me," Jim agreed with a nod, a finger touching his broad-brimmed hat in a farewell salute before he put the jeep in gear and it sprang away.

After watching the jeep disappear, followed by slowly dissipating clouds of dust, Diana turned her gaze in the opposite direction toward the rutted lane that would soon be bringing her husband home. How she was looking forward to that!

Late that afternoon Diana left the stillness of the house for the more companionable sounds of the stables. She had had enough of her own company, and the anticipation of Lije's arrival made the minutes spent alone drag interminably.

An ecstatic whinny greeted her as she paused at the end of the individual enclosures that extended from the outside stall doors. A faint smile of surprise curved her mouth as she saw a sorrel head with a white stripe stretch inquiringly over the rails. There appeared to be such a welcoming eagerness in the horse's face that Diana had to laugh.

"Hello to you, too, Bambi, if that's really what you were saying." She climbed the main fence and made her way down the path to the sorrel's pen. The horse lowered its head for her caress, blowing gently against Diana's bare arm in what seemed like contentment. "If I were really sure that you're as gentle as you seem, I might be persuaded to learn to ride. Not that I'm afraid of horses—" she stroked the shiny neck "—but you must admit, Bambi, that you're awfully far away from the ground!"

The perked ears of the horse swiveled alertly to catch every nuance of Diana's crooning voice. She perched herself on the fence rail while the sorrel explored her arms and legs and face with its nose, inhaling deeply as if memorizing her scent for future reference. Diana continued talking to the horse, unmindful of what she was saying. It didn't seem to matter to the horse, either, as long as her soft voice was heard.

When Diana glanced at her watch nearly an hour and a half later, she was stunned that the time had passed so swiftly. The hour had arrived to feed the horses as she had promised Jim she would do. The sorrel whickered forlornly when Diana climbed down from the top rail.

"It's time to eat, Bambi." She laughed as the horse pushed its head against her chest and kept it there for more gentle caresses. She gave the silken neck one last hug before retracing her steps to the main fence, then on to the barn.

The clanging of the metal buckets as Diana prepared to measure the grain into them was a sufficient signal to the rest of the horses that feeding time had arrived. Instantly they were in their stalls, heads hanging over in anticipation of their evening meal. She didn't have the efficiency of experience that Jim had and it took her longer to complete the filling of the buckets. But soon they were all contentedly munching the grain while Diana went in search of the bales of hay to top off their meal.

Usually there was a stack of bales near the door, but it had been depleted to only two, not enough to feed all the horses. Diana had just placed a foot on the first rung of the ladder leading to the loft when a horn sounded in the yard, followed by "Hello! Is anybody here?"

She walked quickly to the open barn door, brushing away the wisps of loose hay that clung to her wheat tan slacks. Ty Spalding was standing beside the driver's side of his car, his gaze searching the house and yard before spotting Diana standing in the open double doors of the barn.

"Hi, beautiful!" he called, his lithe stride quickly carrying him toward her.

"Hello, Ty," she answered calmly, deliberately not matching his familiar enthusiasm. "What brings you here so late in the day?"

"I was just out at the drilling site." He stopped in front of her, his thoughtful eyes taking in her reserved expression. "I thought I'd stop by and let you know we hit water."

"Lije will be glad to hear that." A partial smile curved her lips.

"Yes." But there was an uncaring sound in his affirmative response. "I stopped up at the house first. When you weren't there, I was about ready to decide that these wide open spaces had finally got to you."

"They can be daunting at times to a city girl." Her gaze shifted from his smiling face to the unending spread of country, remembering the isolated feeling that often attacked her, but for some reason didn't this time.

"East is east and west is west and the wrong one I have chose, as the saying goes." He watched her reaction closely. His comment had found its mark. It was a thought that she had often considered unconsciously and discarded just as often when offset by her love for Lije. "You wouldn't be the first woman to loathe this land or this life," he added.

"What makes you think I do?" she asked noncommitally.

"Instinct. Or maybe—" his brown eyes slowly

traveled the length of her slender but curvaceous frame "—it's just that you seem out of place here. A woman like you should have a more glamorous setting. A classy home in the best section of town with furs and jewels and satin gowns, instead of this." His hand moved in a dismissive gesture to encompass the buildings and land.

"A hybrid rose among yucca plants," Diana concluded for him with a bitter laugh, Jim Two Pony's analogy springing quickly to mind.

"Something like that, yes." There was the barest lifting of one eyebrow. "What made you say that?"

"Oh, it was just a comment I heard someone say once," she shrugged.

"About you?"

"I don't recall." The coolness in her voice indicated that it was time for the subject to be changed.

"Well, in my opinion, you're very much like a rose. A pale yellow tea rose, fragile and delicate and velvety soft to the touch. Not at all like a yucca plant—" a wide grin spread over his face "—with its spindly stalk and greenish white flowers."

"I don't know. It might be apt. After all, I am a greenhorn to this part of the country," she said coolly, more in an effort to disprove his statement than dismiss his compliment.

"That may be, but somehow I could never imagine anyone as lovely as you are compared with something as commonplace as a yucca bush."

"It's nice to be considered functional as well as

ornamental, like a yucca plant is," Diana replied.

"What do you mean? How is a yucca plant functional?" Ty asked with a derisive chuckle.

"I understood its leaves were used to make baskets and clothes."

"By Indians," he said contemptuously. "Not by white people."

"I didn't realize it made any difference. Your prejudice is showing, Ty," she mocked.

"I've never met an Indian yet that was worth anything." A flush of red spread up from his neck at her biting retort. "They're mostly a bunch of drunken bums, an untrustworthy pack of thieves."

"The same thing could apply to some white men I've met," she retorted icily, sickened by his unreasonable bias. "Your description certainly doesn't fit Jim. Lije couldn't have found a more loyal friend than he is."

"Are you actually defending him?" A cynical smirk distorted his mouth. "I imagine that Indian regrets the day you married Lije. It would be amusing to hear what kind of tales he tells Lije about you when you're not around. He's one person who would probably be very happy to see the two of you split up."

His comment was very close to Diana's own initial thoughts about Jim, and her uncomfortable agreement was revealed in her face for a brief second, but long enough for Ty to see. And he didn't hesitate to seize on it. "There's no telling what conjecture his devious mind put on our innocent cup of coffee yesterday. I'm sure he's taking his watchdog duties very seriously."

"I think you're mistaken about Jim." But her voice lacked certainty.

Jim Two Pony had made his dislike of her too apparent in the beginning, at least in her way of thinking. And there was no telling just how much his opinion had mellowed, even though the events of the last couple of days seemed to indicate that it might have.

Ty knew his remarks had touched a vulnerable spot and he also knew when to back away when his point had been made. He very wisely chose that moment to change the subject.

"I'm curious. What brought you down here to the barn at this time of day?"

It took Diana a full second to refocus the direction of her thoughts before she could answer. "I came down to feed the horses."

"You?" There was a light teasing sparkle in his voice and eyes that was reminiscent of the flirtatious side of his personality that she was accustomed to seeing.

"Why not?" she retorted, knowing that two days ago she would have voiced the same disbelief that he had just done.

Ty pushed his hat farther back on his brown head. "Let's just say that I can't visualize you mucking out the stables."

"In other words, you don't think I belong to the horsey set." Laughter danced unwillingly in her eyes.

There was no doubt that Ty Spalding had a considerable amount of charm. A moment ago she had been appalled and angered by his attitude toward Indians in general and Jim Two Pony specifically. Now she found it difficult to remain indifferent to the pleasant side of his personality, perhaps because his marked attention was such a boost to her morale, which had suffered some damaging blows these past weeks.

"I've met some girls who definitely belong in the horsey group," he grinned.

"Such as?"

"Such as Patty King."

"I met her," Diana murmured, blinking her bewilderment at Ty. That was the name of the girl she had met in the restaurant with Lije. "She was a very lovely girl. You could hardly describe her as horsey."

"You met her, did you?" His question was purely rhetorical. "She had her rope all shaken out ready to throw the loop over Lije."

"I...I had the impression that she was fond of him."

"Fond of him!" Ty hooted. "That girl joined the rodeo just to be near him. Your marriage must have been quite a blow to her."

Unbidden the thought came to Diana that if Patty had married Lije she probably would have been out on the range working right beside him instead of sitting in the house always waiting for him to come back.

"I suppose it was a surprise to her," she agreed,

straightening a bit as she spoke. "I haven't finished feeding the horses yet, Ty, so if you'll excuse me, it's getting late."

"What have you got left? I'll help." He was already starting through the open doors of the barn before Diana could reply.

"There's really no need," she said, following him inside the dimly lit building.

"I insist," he smiled. "You make a very beautiful stablehand, but—" his hand reached out to capture one of hers "—I don't like the thought of these lovely hands being soiled or a nail being broken."

"Don't be silly," she responded, snatching her hand away from his grasp. "I'm just as capable of doing this kind of work as anyone else, and a little dirt never hurt anyone."

"Well, I'll help anyway." He teased at the half-angry expression on her face. "What's left to be done?"

It was obvious to Diana that, short of ordering Ty to leave, she wasn't going to persuade him to leave by any subtle method. Although she disliked his attitude toward Jim, he could be extraordinarily pleasant when he tried, and he was a friend of Lije. Heaven knew she had done quite enough to alienate her husband lately, and he wouldn't take kindly to her being rude to one of his friends. So with a resigned sigh she accepted the situation.

"I've already given them their grain. All that's left is the hay."

"Those two bales won't be enough," he observed, glancing at the hay near the door.

"I know," she agreed sharply. "I was just climbing the ladder to the loft to get some more when you came."

"I'll do that while you ration out what's down here."

Reluctantly Diana nodded agreement, walking over to the bales of hay as Ty climbed the ladder to the loft. The horses stamped restlessly in their stalls behind her, lending urgency to her fingers as she pulled at the twine holding the hay in its bales. Above her she could hear Ty walking toward the far end of the loft and she could see the hay chaff sifting through the floorboards of the loft. By the time she had distributed the first two bales Ty had tossed down more. Diana had just freed one of the bales from its twine and was turning to carry the hay to the horses when her feet became entangled in the wiry rope. With a gasping yelp of surprise she went tumbling to the floor. Ty ignored the ladder, swinging from the opening to drop to the floor beside her.

"Are you hurt?" he asked, kneeling beside her.

"No," she answered with a shaky laugh.

The hay that had been in her hands was strewn on and around her. "You look like a scarecrow with that hay sticking out all over you," Ty laughed, assured that she was unharmed.

Now that the surprise of her fall had diminished, Diana was able to join in with his laughter with more merriment. She willingly placed her hand in the one he had extended to her. His hold tightened to pull her to her feet, but the silhouette that loomed in the doorway, blocking out what light the sun offered, halted both their movements. It took Diana only a split second to recognize the tall, masculine figure.

"Lije!" she gasped, scrambling to her feet without the aid of Ty's hand.

"What are you doing here, Spalding?" Lije ignored Diana, quelling the movement she had made toward him with a wintry iron glance.

"I was giving Di—your wife a hand with the horses." Ty's former confidence eluded him in the face of the bristling rancher.

"I'll furnish whatever help my wife needs." Deliberate emphasis was placed on the two words *my wife*.

"Did you just get back?" Her question sounded so nonsensical in the face of such an obvious answer, but Diana felt she had to say something. It was clear that Lije was putting a completely different construction on the innocent scene he had just witnessed. "We didn't expect you back until tomorrow."

By "we," Diana had meant herself and Jim Two Pony. At the narrowing of her husband's gaze she immediately wished she had been more explicit, and she felt herself reddening at his look.

"That's rather obvious, isn't it?" he drawled coldly.

At his insinuation, the hair on the back of her neck began to rise with her temper. For a moment she stood silently in front of him, her back rigid with anger. "Ty was helping me," Diana asserted sharply.

"I think you should go up to the house and start supper." His own anger was barely in check.

"It's getting late," Ty inserted uncertainly. "I'd better be getting along, too."

"It's strange that that thought should just occur to you now." The uncompromising expression on Lije's face was turned on Ty. "I think you'd better stay here for a few more minutes." His cold gray eyes turned once again on Diana. "I thought I told you to go up to the house."

"Yes, you did," she spat out sarcastically. "But, at the time, I didn't realize that I was one of your slaves to be ordered around!"

She saw the fire flash in his eyes as she stalked past him out the door. How dared he treat her that way! Did he have so little faith in her that he thought she would be fooling around the minute he was gone? If Lije thought for one minute, Diana muttered to herself as she strode furiously toward the house, that she was going to be one of those meek little wives who didn't have any backbone to stand up for themselves, then he had another think coming!

Unwillingly Ty's comment about Jim Two Pony came to mind, regarding the things he could have told Lije about her. Jim knew that Ty had been to the house for coffee and Jim had also been the one who had talked to Lije on the telephone the day before. It was possible that he was the one who had placed the doubts about her in Lije's mind.

She hated to concede the possibility, but she had always believed that Jim didn't really want her on the ranch. A sob of pure pain rose in her throat. She had just begun to think that Jim was her friend, but it had all been a ruse, a trick.

When Diana reached the house, tears of frustration and despair were tumbling out of her blue eyes. Why was she letting herself be put through this torture, she wondered. She hated this house and the isolation and desolation of this land! She hated the loneliness of her existence! Why was she going on if her husband didn't even trust her?

"It's time for supper," she mimicked sarcastically, removing pots and pans from the cupboard and flinging them on the stove top. "What am I, a maid?" she demanded into the air.

There was satisfaction in the vicious rattling of the pans. With the back of her hand Diana scrubbed the betraying tears of softness from her cheeks. She wouldn't give Lije the satisfaction of seeing her cry.

Her back was to the door when she heard it open and close. She kept it that way even when she heard Lije's footsteps carry him farther into the room.

"Supper won't be ready for another half hour, sir." Diana added the last with a decidedly sarcastic note.

"Damn the supper!" His hand gripped her arm and spun her around to face him. His expression was ruthlessly cold. "What I want is an explanation."

"I don't owe you an explanation," she retorted through gritted teeth.

"I'm gone for three days. I rush back here to apologize for not understanding and find my wife stretched out in the hay with another man, and you have the nerve to say you don't owe me an explanation!" The temper that had been firmly controlled before now ran unchecked.

"That's exactly what I am saying!" Diana let her anger flare, too, as her flashing blue eyes clashed with the rolling thunderclouds in his gray ones.

"I knew you were lonely out here—" an ominous quiet crept into his voice "—but I never dreamed you were so desperate for attention as to do this."

Diana never thought she would see the glittering contempt that was now in her husband's face. And the pain it caused her heart was unbelievable. She had to strike back.

"Yes, I've been lonely," she cried. "Who wouldn't be lonely in this godforsaken hole? There's nothing to see, nowhere to go, nobody to talk to, just nothing! And I hate it! Do you hear me? I hate it!"

Now both of his hands were gripping her shoulders, his fingers digging into the bone. "You knew what it was like. I told you," he growled fiercely, giving her a shake that made her teeth rattle.

"There aren't any adequate words to describe the desolation of this place," she declared, refusing to flinch at the physical pain she was experiencing at his hands.

"This is my land, my home."

"Congratulations," she said sarcastically. "You and Jim are welcome to it."

"Jim!" he snarled. "I wondered when you'd bring his name into this. You never could stand him, could you? He's a Navaho and not quite human."

"You've always refused to accept the fact that Jim doesn't like me," Diana accused him. "You would take his word over mine anytime, wouldn't you?"

"At least he isn't as prejudiced as you are," Lije retorted, letting his disgust coat his words with bitter paint. "Or as disloyal."

"I can't stand any more of this." Her anger gave way to sobs of frustration as she twisted to free herself from his grasp. "You don't even try to understand how I feel! You don't even care!"

"And I suppose Ty Spalding does," he sneered, releasing his hold and stepping away as if she were contaminated.

"He's not like you. He's human. He's capable of making mistakes." Her chin trembled as much as her voice.

"Well—" Lije sighed heavily as his gaze roamed over her with cold disregard "—I made one hell of a mistake when I married you."

It felt as if a knife had been plunged in her heart and Diana gasped at the pain.

"It's a miracle you don't blame me for that, too," she said bitterly. "After all, you were content to say goodbye and move on to another rodeo.

I was the one who so stupidly refused to accept your decision.''

''Hindsight is always more enlightening. But it doesn't do any good to say 'what if we hadn't got married?' We did and we are. The only thing that remains to be done is to get unmarried.'' Lije said it so casually and matter-of-factly. ''You can forget about supper. You'll have plenty of time to pack your things tonight. Jim can take you into town tomorrow. Have your lawyer get hold of me.''

Diana was still standing in the same place when Lije walked out the door.

CHAPTER TWELVE

LIJE DID NOT come back to the house that night. Diana could only presume that he was staying in Jim Two Pony's cabin. Pride wouldn't allow her to go in search of him, to beg his forgiveness when she was guilty of nothing—except perhaps of loving him too much and having too much pride. And, in spite of the accusations she had flung at him, she did love him. But did it do any good? Had she and Lije come up against an obstacle that not even their love could surmount? Was it, as he had once said, love at the wrong place and the wrong time?

Diana went through the motions of preparing her own evening meal and even sat down at the table with the intention of eating, but her fork succeeded mostly in pushing the food around on her plate. Very few morsels actually made it to her mouth. It was doubly strange to clear the table and wash the dishes with the thought always at the back of her mind that this was the last time she would be doing it. The kitchen that had always seemed so distasteful to her aesthetic eye suddenly seemed very homely. It was hard to visualize any other life.

She wandered through the rest of the house, telling herself all the time how lucky she was to be able to leave its dismal interior, but she did a terrible job of convincing herself. It didn't seem true that she was really leaving. Not even when her suitcases were dragged from the closet and lay open on the bed did it seem possible that she was. The whole thing took on the aspect of a bad dream. Diana kept thinking that any moment Lije would walk through the door and the cold ache in the area of her heart would melt away at the sight of him. But he never came.

Mechanically she filled the suitcases, her thoughts taking off on peculiar tangents considering the situation. When she removed a long hostess skirt from the closet, its rich nutty gold color sent her wondering what the pillows on the living room sofa would look like covered in this mutedly brilliant shade. Before she realized what she was doing, she had carried the skirt into the living room to wrap it around one of the pillows. The effect against the brown tweed sofa was amazing. There was just enough light yellow in the material to add brightness to the room and still blend with the existing furniture. Why hadn't she thought of it before?

And again, a few minutes later, she picked up a blue silk neckscarf that had a plain border of white daisies around it. The simplicity of the flower design brought an instantaneous inspiration to decorate the metal cupboards in the kitchen by edging the cupboard doors with flowers. The Danish decor could be carried through by redoing the kitchen table and chair. New curtains at the window and fresh paint on the walls would. . . .

Diana put a firm brake on her thoughts. She was leaving. Lije had told her to go. Their marriage was over. Why did she persist with these thoughts about a house she would never live in again after tonight?

Very slowly, a tear trickled out of each eye until soon Diana's cheeks were deluged by the outpouring. She was entitled to a good cry, she told herself as she clicked the last suitcase shut. She had a right to cry. Hadn't her husband, the only man she could ever love, accused her wrongly of being unfaithful? Hadn't he ordered her around like some unfeeling servant? Hadn't Jim Two Pony plotted from the beginning to rid the ranch of her? She had a right to cry! But she also remembered very vividly and very guiltily that she had told Lije she hated the ranch and her life on it.

The morning sun found a tear-drenched pillow, and suitcases piled beside the kitchen door. Diana sat at the table, staring at the cup of black coffee out of eyes that were ringed with dark circles. There weren't any more tears left. She felt drained of all emotion, a hollow shell of a person with nothing left inside to feel pain or anguish.

An hour before, she had seen Lije from the kitchen window walking across the ranch yard to crawl into the jeep. He hadn't even glanced toward the house. As he drove out of sight, the last thread of hope that there would be a reconciliation faded out of sight with him. There wasn't even going to be a last goodbye.

The soft catlike tread on the porch floor announced the arrival of Jim Two Pony to take her away from the ranch. Diana inhaled deeply as he walked through the door, drawing her protective armor of pride more securely around her before she raised her head to meet his gaze. She expected to see gloating triumph written on his smugly complacent face, but certainly not the gentle sympathy that showed so boldly in his dark eyes. It very nearly banished her shield of pride.

"My suitcases are there by the door," she said sharply. "You might as well begin carrying them out to the truck."

"Are you sure you want me to?" Jim asked quietly, his black eyes never leaving her face.

"Well, I'm certainly not about to carry them all." Deliberately misunderstanding his question, Diana rose to her feet. Jim hesitated for a minute more before reaching down to pick up two of the larger cases. After slipping on her jacket Diana reached for her purse, then followed him out the door.

"Where are you going?"

"It doesn't really matter, does it?" Diana answered coldly, not seeing any need to carry on a civil conversation with someone who was probably glad to see her go. "It's enough of a pleasure to be leaving this godforsaken piece of country."

"That may have been true once, when you first came." He glanced at her sideways. "But if you are honest with yourself, you don't feel that way about the ranch now."

The ironic truth of his words sent a wave of pain through her heart. A whinny from the stable area intensified it. She would never see her pretty Bambi horse again, either. But Diana didn't let her mask of cold indifference slip. That mask and her pride were her only defense against the unbearable agony that was just below the surface.

"Don't be a hypocrite, Jim. Not at this late date. I know you're quite happy to see me go."

"Why should I be?"

"Don't be obtuse," Diana said scathingly. "You made it plain from the beginning that you didn't think I belonged here. You should be rejoicing that you were proved right."

"I'm sorry. I don't know what you are talking about." He set the luggage in the back of the pickup and turned to look at her.

"Oh, surely you recall our conversation in the barn shortly after I came here," she said mockingly. "That brilliant story about the yucca plant and the rose. You don't really think I'm so dense that I didn't ralize that you were telling me I was the rose? And roses don't take kindly to transplanting, especially city roses."

"You misunderstood the point of what I was telling you." Jim shook his head sadly. "I was trying to explain that you had to choose which you were going to be, useful and self-sufficient like the yucca or decorative and pampered like the rose. Surely it's obvious from the way you've always pitched in without a complaint, even to helping with the horses, that you are a yucca flower."

"I don't understand," Diana whispered. She wanted to doubt his words, but the sincerity in his voice was too marked. "Why were you so cold to me? You would barely even talk to me unless I forced you."

"I...." He paused in search of the right words. "I don't make friends easily. Partly, I admit, because I am a Navaho and few white people are really interested in being my friend, let alone a white woman. I couldn't know at the beginning whether you were feeling sorry for me or were just being patronizing. We Navaho have a lot of pride. It isn't a commodity restricted only to you."

"Oh, Jim, I wish I'd known that before," she murmured.

"Was I part of your argument with Lije?"

"Part," she admitted. Her head was downcast so that her silvery fair hair hid her face before she tossed her head and sent it cascading down her back. "Lije believes I'm prejudiced against you because you're a Navaho. He couldn't understand that I thought you didn't like me or want me here—probably because he knew you better."

"Then your leaving is my fault."

"No." She reached out and touched his arm. "No, it isn't. We quarreled because of Ty Spalding. Lije thought...." Diana couldn't bring herself to voice what he thought; but even unspoken, Jim knew. "But I suppose he told you all about it."

"He didn't speak of it to me. Although he did seem surprised when I told him you had fed the horses. I remember he muttered, 'So that's what she was doing in the barn.'"

"I'd tripped over some baling twine and Ty was helping me up when Lije walked in," she murmured, a haunting look in her eyes as she glanced at the barn.

"And you didn't explain?"

"I was so hurt—" a sob crept into her voice "—that he could believe I would do what he thought I was doing. I'm afraid I can be very stubborn," she said with a half laugh. "Later when he asked me to explain, I...I refused. That's when we really started quarreling. And—" Diana looked out over the expansive horizon, shimmering in golden sunlight with a suggestion of spring green "—and that's when I told him how much I hated living here. It's really ironic, Jim, but for so long I've thought I didn't like it—being out here so alone and cut off from everybody—that I don't even know when I really did stop hating it and started liking it. It wrapped me in its spell. Lije once told me that it was called the 'land of enchantment.'"

Jim reached into the back end of the pickup truck and took out the two suitcases he had just placed in there.

"What are you doing?" Diana asked as he started walking toward the house with them.

"I'm not taking you anywhere," Jim said firmly. A smile took some of the harshness out of his voice. "If Lije wants you to leave, then he's going to have to take you himself. And if I were you, I would tell him exactly what you told me—if you still love him, which I think you do."

"I wouldn't know where to begin."

"An apology is usually effective." He set one of the suitcases down and held the door open for Diana. She stepped inside, expecting Jim to follow, but he only placed the bags inside and walked back out.

"Where are you going?" she called after him.

"I thought I would let Lije know there's someone here at the house who wants to speak to him," Jim answered with a decided twinkle in his eyes.

"Thank you seems like such a little thing to say to you, Jim," Diana said softly, the screen door shading her face so he couldn't see the diamond-bright glitter of tears intensifying the blue of her eyes.

"Don't thank me yet," he laughed. "You haven't talked to Lije."

The rumbling roar of an accelerating motor attracted Jim and Diana. Both turned toward the sound to see the jeep bouncing over the uneven ground to the ranch yard. Only one person was in the vehicle and both of them knew it was Lije. Diana stood silently just inside the screen door, unconsciously holding her breath.

"Don't let him see you," Jim said in a sotto voice meant for her alone when the jeep stopped beside the pickup truck with Lije hopping out almost before the motor stopped turning over.

Diana stepped away from the door as she saw Lije's long strides eating the distance between the jeep and the house.

"Where's Diana?" he demanded harshly.

"Why?" Jim asked calmly.

"Because I want to see her. Now, dammit, where did you take her? To the bus station?" Lije made no attempt to conceal his impatience, and Diana wished she could see his face.

"No." Jim sounded remarkably unruffled, she thought, considering the leashed violence in Lije's voice.

"Then where?" he nearly shouted.

"I didn't take her anywhere," Jim said calmly.

It was as if the whole world had come to a halt, so profound was the silence. Slowly Diana stepped in front of the screen door to look at her husband, whose head had been thrown back in surprise while his whole attention became focused on the door.

"I'm right here, Lije," she said quietly.

Their gazes met and locked through the mesh of the screen. Jim glanced back at Diana briefly before silently stepping past Lije and walking away. Again Diana experienced that strange communication with the gray eyes that she had felt when they first met. Without conscious volition, her hand reached down and opened the screen door for Lije to enter.

"Did you want to see me?" she asked.

"Yes," he said, but he made no move toward the opened door.

"I hope you didn't come to say goodbye, Lije, because I'm not leaving," Diana began. He still had that terrible mask of remoteness on his face. There was no indication whether he was pleased or angry by her statement, so she rushed on. "At least, I'm not going until I've had a chance to tell you that I didn't mean any of those things I said yesterday. And...and I...I still love you. I'll always love you, Lije." Something that looked like pain flickered across the strong bronzed lines of his face. "I don't hate the ranch. At first I admit everything was strange and I was lonely, but it's not true anymore. I guess I said that to hurt you and I'm sorry. As for what happened in the barn with Ty, I want to explain about—"

"No!" The word exploded in the air as he covered the distance between them in one lithe move. His hands gripped her shoulders as he simultaneously stepped farther into the house and pulled her tightly against his chest. "Don't say any more, Diana," he murmured, his voice muffled in the silken softness of her hair. "I can't bear for you to humble yourself any more when I'm the one who should be on his knees begging you to forgive me. I know exactly what happened in the barn yesterday."

"How?" Diana twisted her head to look at him in a mixture of disbelief and happiness.

"I just had a long talk with Spalding at the drilling site. I was too angry yesterday to do more than order him to stay away from you." He smiled down at her with that smile that could always take her breath away. She would have spoken, but he covered her mouth with his hand. "I know all about your tripping over the twine. Nothing I can say justifies my failure to trust you. The only way I can explain why I acted the way I did was that I was jealous. I was outside when I heard you laugh. Darling, do you have any idea how long it has been since I heard you laugh? Not since the first day I brought you here. When I walked into the barn and saw you with Ty and realized that he had made you laugh, when I had failed, I was crazy with jealousy and anger. Can you ever forgive me?"

"Oh, Lije!" She kissed the tips of his fingers, which had begun caressing her face. "If you can forgive me for the way I hurt you—"

"I deserved it," he murmured, gathering her closer in his arms. "But that's why I came looking for you—so you would know that I knew the truth. If I could I was going to persuade you to come back."

"And I was half-afraid you were going to be angry because I was still here," she laughed shortly.

"I love you, Diana." He looked deep into her eyes. "I could never let you go, even if I knew I was making your life miserable. That's how selfish I am."

"If you don't hurry up and kiss me, you're going to make my life very miserable," she teased.

"You little witch!" Lije laughed. Then he proceeded to kiss her thoroughly, making up for those empty days and empty nights when he had been gone, sweeping her off into a vortex of ever rising passion until neither one was satisfied with the physical restrictions of their embrace. "We have a lot of lost time to make up for, Diana," he whispered against the hollow of her neck.

"Yes," she agreed fervently, her mouth bruised by the fierceness of his kisses even as she yearned for it to be reclaimed by his.

"Shall we do something about it now?" He lifted his head from hers to gaze down into her eyes, their lids heavy with the ardency of his lovemaking.

"Yes," she breathed, then, "no, I mean...."

"What do you mean?" he laughed softly, amused by her shaky voice.

"There's something else I want to do first," she murmured.

"What's that?" A frown creased his forehead.

Diana took his hand and led him outside. There she walked over and grabbed the thick rope that hung from the metal bell.

"Where did that come from?" Lije asked as Diana began pulling the clapper so that the bell rang loudly in the quiet countryside.

"Jim hung it for me while you were gone," she said with a beaming smile. Down at one of the small sheds, she saw Jim Two Pony step into the open, his hand waving in recognition of the bell. She waved back before walking over to her husband and putting her arms around his waist. "You do know that Jim refused to take me away from here, don't you?"

"I received that impression." Lije smiled.

"I thought it was only fair to let him know that all is well between us. After all, Jim is *our* best friend." She gazed earnestly up at her husband. "And I do mean that, Lije."

"I'm glad," he said softly, his eyes glinting with pride and love. Then he was sweeping her off her feet and cradling her in his arms. "Shall we go home, Mrs. Masters?"

"I think it's about time, Mr. Masters," she smiled. Her arms encircled his neck as he once again carried her over the threshold.

You'll flip . . . your pages won't!
Read paperbacks *hands-free* with

Book Mate • I

The perfect "mate" for all your romance paperbacks

Traveling • Vacationing • At Work • In Bed • Studying
• Cooking • Eating

Perfect size for all standard paperbacks, this wonderful invention makes reading a pure pleasure! Ingenious design holds paperback books OPEN and FLAT so even wind can't ruffle pages — leaves your hands free to do other things. Reinforced, wipe-clean vinyl-covered holder flexes to let you turn pages without undoing the strap . . . supports paperbacks so well, they have the strength of hardcovers!

Pages turn WITHOUT opening the strap

SEE-THROUGH STRAP

Reinforced back stays flat

Built in bookmark

BOOK MARK

BACK COVER HOLDING STRIP

10" x 7¼ opened
Snaps closed for easy carrying, too

Available now. Send your name, address, and zip code, along with a check or money order for just $5.95 + .75¢ for delivery (for a total of $6.70) payable to Reader Service to:

Reader Service
Bookmate Offer
3010 Walden Avenue
P.O. Box 1396
Buffalo, N.Y. 14269-1396

Offer not available in Canada
*New York residents add appropriate sales tax.

BM-GR